Copyright © 2022 by Mara Webb

All rights reserved. No part of this publication may be reproduced, distributed, or transmitted in any form or by any means, including photocopying, recording, or other electronic or mechanical methods, without the prior written permission of the publisher, except in the case of brief quotations embodied in critical reviews and certain other noncommercial uses permitted by copyright law.

A SCONE TO PICK

COMPASS COVE COZY MYSTERY BOOK 5

MARA WEBB

CHAPTER 1

"Zora? Zora, are you paying attention?" Amos asked me.

I sat up straight in my chair, trying to pretend that I hadn't been sleeping. "I am paying attention, I am!"

Amos put his hands on his hips and looked at me in a disbelieving way. "Perhaps you can just recap what I was saying then? If one wants to perform a pushing spell with great urgency you would use the incantation…"

"*Forca Apasati*," I said, answering the question easily, even though I *had* been sleeping.

"Very good, except that wasn't what I was talking about at all. We're in the middle of a lecture on Magic History—do you recall?" Amos placed his hands upon his desk and looked at me like a disproving mother.

"I… I'm sorry Amos. I don't mean to be disrespectful; I just find it very hard to concentrate in these sessions. This history stuff can be very dry."

He nodded as though he agreed. "You're not entirely wrong, a lot of this material is lacking I agree, unfortunately it is a required part of your education. There's no question that you're a talented witch, Zora, that I can't deny. Since obtaining a working wand you have excelled at the practical element of magic, and you have an amazing ability to retain information, but I'm afraid when it comes to history and theory..."

"I know, I know. I'm... I'm really bad at this bit. Again, I'm sorry."

"Tell you what, let's have a break. It's been about an hour, and my throat is feeling a little dry. Would you like a tea? Coffee?"

"A coffee would be great actually," I said with a long yawn. It might even give me enough energy to get through the rest of this class.

"Alright. Wait here, I'll be back in a minute. Want some cake too?"

"Absolutely," I said.

One month ago, I'd started lessons at Magic School, initially having my classes in a dreary little beige building with two other adults that were deemed as magical 'late-starters'. After a few initial hiccups because of a malfunctioning wand, I found myself moving through the lessons and mastering the basics rather quickly.

I only ended up doing a few lessons at the official venue before Amos took me to one side and recommended that I skip several grades ahead to material that might be more challenging for me. Since then, my lessons had been private one-on-one sessions conducted in the conservatory of Amos' rather impressive Victorian house nestled on its own generous plot on the edge of Compass Cove town.

The Aposhine family, of which Amos was a part of, was a very old wizarding family with a considerable amount of wealth and influence. Amos was an old man with a long white beard and a dark blue suit covered in little crescent moons, but photographs around the large house told stories of his childhood, which he spent in a magical travelling circus with his mother and father.

Despite the size of the house, it was only Amos and his wife here now, and I rarely saw her while I was here for my lessons. Amos had four children who had all grown up and flown from the coop. This was my third time at his house now, having lessons in a large conservatory that overlooked a considerable lawn surrounded by luscious green trees.

"Zora, remind me again," Amos shouted from the kitchen adjacent. "Do you have sugar in your coffee?"

"No, but I expect plenty of sugar in the cake."

Amos chuckled. "No worries there."

It was then that I realized my phone was ringing in my bag. I had a look at the screen and saw it was my sister, Zelda. "Make it quick," I answered, "I'm at Amos' house."

"Ah, I totally forgot you had class tonight. How's it going?" she asked.

"Oh, you know, falling asleep again and embarrassing myself. Is everything okay?"

"I'm... I'm not sure. I just went out to return some books at the library and there's a note on the entrance saying it's closed. The library is *never* closed Zora, it's a magic library."

"Huh, actually I did see that sign a few weeks ago when I went there. I was going to mention it, but it completely slipped my mind. It's still closed?"

"Yeah, by the looks of it. It's seriously unusual Zora, Agnes has never closed the library before, now you're telling me it's been closed for several weeks?" Zelda sounded concerned and rightly so.

The last time we'd been to the library together we'd been kicked out for accidentally breaking into the restricted section. We were trying to find out more about our mother's disappearance. She was one of the only witches in Compass Cove with access to the magic library's restricted section, and we wanted to know why.

I was convinced I'd recently seen my mother for a split-second, hiding in the reflection of my bathroom mirror. After making amends with the head librarian and seeing my mom's borrowing record, it looked very likely that she was trapped inside a magical realm called the mirror dimension—why, we did not know.

After making amends, Agnes, the head librarian, had agreed to show me around the restricted section if I could first help her with a small problem the library had been having. I hadn't actually been able to help her with that problem yet, and something told me the library being closed had something to do with it.

"I think we should investigate," Zelda said. "Something is seriously amiss here, and didn't Agnes say she needed your help?"

"She did, but I never found out why."

"Well, I think it's obvious this is connected. I'm off work tomorrow morning. Let's go and have a look then?"

I sighed. "Fine, but you're buying me a churro on the way."

"You run a bakery, make your own churro," Zelda argued.

"Nah, it tastes better when made by someone else. I want to eat food prepared by someone that doesn't care about my arteries. Does that make sense?"

"…Unfortunately, it does. We may be spending too much time together. Alright, I'll see you at the bakery tomorrow morning. Stay awake in your class!"

"No promises," I muttered and hung up the phone.

Shortly after that Amos returned with cake and coffee. The short snack break certainly revitalized my spirits and that effect doubled when Amos introduced our next topic.

"Okay, I'll be honest," he said as he set down his empty plate. "We can probably skip over some history and theory—the tests are largely practical anyway, so even if you completely flunk the written stuff, you can still pass."

"There's a vote of confidence if I ever heard one," I joked.

"Before we move on though there is one last topic we have to cover, and I'm afraid I can't skip this one at all." Amos was typically quite a jovial fellow, but his voice had taken on a rarer serious quality now.

"Okay…" I said, wondering what would bring about this change in him.

"History of Dark Magic, and its consequences," he said and cleared his throat. Amos snapped his fingers and a projector and screen appeared behind him. He did this sometimes whenever there was a visual element to his lessons. "Try and stay awake now, Zora, this *is* important."

"Don't worry, I will." I sat up straight in my chair and for the first time during that lesson I willingly found myself paying attention. I don't know why the topic intrigued me so, but after a few run ins with dark witches, I was eager to learn more about this side of magic—not so I could employ it, just so I could better defend myself.

"Well then, what do you know about dark magic?" Amos asked as an introductory question.

"Not much to be honest. It's... bad, and it's used by bad people?" I cringed a little, thinking that I sounded like a preschool child offering an overly simple explanation.

"In a brief way it's not a bad description. As things stand there is actually no official definition of what constitutes dark magic, but there are rules within magic, and most of them fall in line with human laws. Do not murder, do not harm or steal. You cannot use magic to obtain wealth you haven't earned; you cannot use magic to influence or manipulate someone against their will. Dark magic effectively then is when one deliberately violates these rules and laws knowingly."

"So how does one become a dark witch or wizard?" I asked. I added quickly, "Out of interest, of course, I'm not thinking of joining up."

"I *do* hear they have great dental cover," Amos said, chuckling at his own joke. "To answer your question however, a dark witch or wizard usually sacrifices a part of their soul to increase their magical power. I'm sure you know by now that there are other realms of existence out there, realities that narrowly border our own. The Astral realms, the Akashic planes, etcetera."

"I've heard a little about them, though I don't know much," I admitted.

"For this topic, all you have to know is this: on those planes there are demons and magical entities, much more powerful than even our strongest witches and wizards. However, as strong as they are, they are not able to exist in our physical plane of existence for any meaningful amount of time, so they are not really a threat."

"But dark witches and wizards use them somehow?" I asked.

"Not quite. It's actually the other way around. The demon or magical entity uses *them*. The dark magic user sacrifices part of their soul to the dark source, and in exchange their patron leaves a small part of their power in them." Amos clicked a small controller in his hand and the slide on the projector changed.

On the screen there was an old painting of a rather terrifying looking woman in a tattered black dress. She was standing on a hill in the midst of a medieval battlefield, a wand held tightly in her hand and an army of men surrounding her, their swords pointed in her direction.

"Dark magicians turn up around once a century or so," Amos explained. "They don't appear often, because they are usually witches and wizards of very exceptional ability. More often than not they are women, as women have a more natural affinity for magic."

"Who is she?" I asked, looking at the chilling scene on the screen. The woman was pale white, with mottled black hair and bright emerald eyes that almost seemed luminescent. She looked feral.

"Layla the Terrible, her reign of terror ran from 1502-1512. In the last millennium she is one of the strongest witches to have ever lived. During her tyranny she killed thousands, and for a significant time she had the entire world in her palm."

I leaned forward. "Wait a second, I've heard about her."

Amos nodded as though this was normal. "Yes, she's quite infamous, I've no doubt you have heard something about her by now."

"No, I mean—" Darn, how did I even explain this? A few weeks ago, when I was testing out my new wand, I accidentally summoned something called an *oracle*, a magical talking skull with flaming blue eyes. After telling me he was here to stay he insisted that I *had* to name him. I went with 'Fancy Bill', and he told me that his last master had been a dark witch named 'Layla the Terrible.'

"Zora?" Amos prompted, after I spent a few seconds too long trying to put together my thoughts.

"Do you know what an oracle is? Why am I asking? Of course you do, you're a magical teacher."

Amos laughed at my machine-gun fire word vomit and nodded his head. "I am familiar with them, yes. Why do you ask?"

"A few weeks ago, I accidentally summoned one when letting off some surplus magical energy. I hadn't used magic properly for a few days because my wand was broken, and when my cousin Sabrina brought me a replacement it felt like I was about to blow."

Amos blinked in amazement. "I'm sorry, you summoned an oracle? Are you sure?"

"Yes," I said with a sigh. "He's the real deal. Anyway, he told me his last master had been a dark witch named Layla the Terrible."

My magic teacher's eyes widened even further. "Oh my, that is... *quite* unusual. Zora as a prismatic witch I expect your abilities to outperform in unexpected ways, but summoning an oracle, and by accident at that, *that* is highly impressive, unprecedented one might even say."

"He says he's neutral," I said as way of assurance. "That oracles don't have an affiliation either way, they just do what they're told. He's not good or evil."

"Yes, that's right, I don't think you have any reason to fear. In fact, you have inherited a very useful assistant. An oracle can apparently access all the knowledge in the universe, but it can take them time to find their answers."

"Well, I've accidentally set him the task of looking up idioms and expressions. I don't really know how to get him to stop. In fact, he won't stop."

He nodded again. "Yes, that's quite normal from what I've read about them. They are literal and will pursue a task until it is complete. I must say I would very much like a chance to see this unusual creature if I ever get the chance."

"Feel free to come to the bakery whenever. He's very mouthy."

"I bet..." he said and laughed in bewilderment. "Anyway, back to our matter at hand. After Layla the Terrible, another dark witch appeared in Scotland about a century later, she called herself Hovan the Destroyer, and she actually styled herself after her predecessor."

Amos clicked to a new slide, showing an old painting of a red-haired girl with blue face paint. "Fortunately, her reign didn't last long—she was burned at the stake before she did any real damage," he said.

"Yikes."

"Then we had Isabella Mort, a particularly nasty sorceress.

Following her were Charlie and Francesca Lupin, who called themselves 'The Twins of Fate'. After that, things were quiet for a few centuries, until—" With another click a new slide came into focus, this one showing an unassuming photograph of an ordinary man with short dark hair, a hook nose and piercing dark eyes. "Richard Desmond."

"Who?" I asked.

Amos repeated the name. "Born in 1960, originally from a small settlement not too far from Compass Cove. From birth it was evident Desmond was an extremely gifted wizard, his abilities far surpassing that of his peers. He quickly rose through the ranks of our world and became a man of great power and influence, ultimately becoming the Sorcerer Supreme of all magical kind after winning an election in 1995, just after his 35th birthday."

"I thought this section was about dark witches and wizards?" I reminded Amos.

He cleared his throat. "It is. After that, things took a turn. A dark one." Amos brought up the next slide, on this one there was a photograph of a town on fire, and at the very top of the picture the chilling silhouette of a lone man. I don't know why, but the image sent a shiver through me.

"What happened?" I asked.

"Some dark source consumed him, and a man that was formerly lauded and respected across the magical world, became a great and terrible tyrant. His influence and his armies spread fast, and just when he was about to take control of everything… he vanished."

"He vanished?"

"That's right. Twenty-three years ago. No one knows where he went. His followers quickly disbanded, and a balance returned to our magical world. Ever since then we have been at peace but know this—the temptation of darkness is strong for those who have the power, and even a witch that is strong of heart can lose her way."

After a few moments of quiet reflection, I looked up at Amos and realized something. "This isn't a part of the standard syllabus, is it?" I asked.

He shook his head. "No, this topic is of my own curation," he said, holding my gaze. "Your powers are still growing, Zora Wick, but your powers are astonishingly strong, especially for the amount of time—"

"Is that why we're having this conversation?" I asked, feeling slightly annoyed. "You think I'm going to become like these people? You think I'd move to the dark side?"

He held his hands up as though I'd got it wrong. "Not at all, I'm just warning you. I do not say this lightly Zora, in all my years I've only ever seen one other with your ability. And it does scare me in a way. You *are* a good person, and I'm not suggesting anything else. But that doesn't change the fact that these dark sources *will* approach you, and they are very gifted when it comes to temptation."

I felt myself cool down a little, realizing it wasn't fair to snap at Amos like that. He was just warning me after all, even if it did feel a little unsettling. "I have no intention of being like those people. Power and greed, it doesn't interest me at all."

Amos offered a weak smile. "One thing is for sure Zora, you will *be* an exceptional witch, I can promise you that. Heed my warning however—there are people and forces out there that will seek to make you an exceptionally dark witch. You have to have your wits about you. I think we'll end the session there tonight."

With that I stood up and felt a million thoughts forming in my head.

Amos had certainly got my attention this lesson, that was for sure. After packing my things up I went to leave but stopped and turned around to ask him one more question. "You said you've only ever seen one other person with my ability. Who?"

"An old student of mine. Unfortunately, his path went astray, and he turned to the darkness."

"Do you mind if I ask who it was?"

"Of course, he was the same man I just told you about, the one who nearly turned our magical world to complete darkness before he vanished. That student's name was Richard Desmond."

CHAPTER 2

Did I really have it in me to be a dark witch? To drive people away and do terrible things?

Before I came to Compass Cove my life felt quite solitary. I had a dead-end job; a small shoebox apartment and my life was rather empty. Growing up it had just been me and my dad, a regular mortal man named Nolan Yates. I missed him terribly since he'd passed, and things had only started to pick up after I inherited my bakery here in Compass Cove.

With the bakery came the discovery that I was a witch, and that my elusive mother had a daughter with another man, meaning that I had a half-sister named Zelda. Zelda was as mad as a box of frogs, but she had a very kind heart and I loved her to bits.

Recently I'd hired several people to help me at the bakery, there was Daphne, an extremely talented witch, but her remarkable baking skills had nothing to do with her magic. She was exceptionally dependable and something of a godsend.

My more recent hire was a chaotic witch name Rosie, an Irish firecracker with a penchant for trouble. Despite her eclectic ways, Rosie knew her way around the kitchen and was a natural when it came to customer service. Since joining the business our sales had permanently bumped because of the repeat customers she brought in.

I had more family in Compass Cove too—my cousins Celeste and Sabrina were sisters despite being opposites in every way. Celeste ran her own café with Zelda, and Sabrina ran a magical shop called *Wytch's Bazaar*. She was also one of the only wand makers in town.

An older woman named Liza was grandmother to all of us, though something of a recluse and rarely seen since I'd moved to town. She had two daughters, Tabitha, mother to Zelda and me, and Constance, mother to Sabrina and Celeste.

Constance was actually murdered a year before I moved to town, and her murder was only solved once I moved here and started poking my nose around. She loved to show up at any opportunity and scare the living daylights out of people. My mother Tabitha vanished mysteriously just after Zelda was born, and no one had seen her until a few weeks ago, when I caught a brief glimpse of her hiding in the reflection of my bathroom mirror. Finding out what had happened to her was on my to-do list and visiting the library with Zelda was an obstacle on the way.

Then of course there was Hudson and Blake, the two knuckle-dragging alpha males that had deemed themselves my protectors since I moved to town. I was a prismatic witch, a rare person with the ability to use all types of magic, and as such two different factions had assigned the protectors to make sure I was safe.

Blake was a werewolf and Hudson was a magically enhanced human that worked for a secret magical organization called MAGE. Up until very recently they'd both hated one another, but after being hit with a curse that meant they couldn't be further than ten feet apart, they'd somehow become best of friends. The friendship persisted even now that the curse was broken.

Part of their hatred had come from this unusual love triangle that existed between us, which ended when Blake very recently became married after a surprise arranged marriage. I still knew very little about the circumstance behind the marriage and only met his wife briefly, a very beautiful woman with long blonde hair, who came from another werewolf pack.

Though the arranged marriage felt like a cloud, there was a silver lining in that it cleared the muddy waters between me and my guardians. Hudson and I had now been dating for several weeks, I was smiling all the time and the relationship hadn't dampened Hudson's friendship with Blake.

Finally, there were the non-human associates I had made since moving to town. I had a familiar named Hermes; he was a little black cat that could talk until the cows came home. Then there was Phoebe, a 'time owl' that resided in a cage in my living room. She was quiet and mostly kept to herself, and at the moment she mostly acted as a pre-emptive caller ID—admittedly I was probably underutilizing her various talents.

The most recent addition to my ever-growing carnival of familiars was 'Fancy Bill', a strange talking skull that apparently knew everything in the universe, but how useful he actually was would remain to be seen.

Since coming here my life was obviously a lot fuller. Some days I could almost scream because things were so hectic, but to be honest I don't think I could ever go back to my life before this. It felt like everyone in this town was crazy, but I couldn't imagine myself being anywhere else now.

I somehow kept falling into murder mysteries and had become somewhat of an unofficial sleuth in town, having earned a reputation as a woman that can't keep her nose out of other peoples' business. One thing was clear, I'd never felt so focused or on the ball. My mind was razor sharp and—

"Zora you're piping buttercream all over your hand," Rosie said with amusement.

"Huh?" Looking down I saw that, sure enough, I *was* piping buttercream all over my hand. I had been filling eclairs and during my absent-minded daydream the éclair had exploded and overflowing with excess filling from the bag. I set them both down on a tray. "Oops."

"Where's your mind at?" Rosie asked as I went over to the sink and washed my hands off. "You've not been involved with any of the banter this morning."

Although the morning bake meant that we started work early—most days we were up and at it by 4am—working with Rosie and Daphne was a joy, and we spent a lot of the time talking and joking around. It was true that I'd been away with the birds this morning. Rosie and Daphne had been chatting away throughout the morning bake and I'd been standing there like a zombie, my thoughts looping endlessly over every facet of my life.

"You *are* unusually quiet," Daphne said with a note of concern. "Anything we need to know?"

"She's convinced she's going to go crazy and kill us all," Zelda said as she walked through the back door.

"Zelda!" I said.

"What? It's true." She looked at Daphne. "She texted me and told me last night after her magic class. Her teacher's convinced she's going to go bonkers and enslave humanity."

"Do you know why I texted that information to you, instead of writing it on the wall for everyone to see?" I asked, hoping Zelda would get the hint.

"...Because you wanted to give me the honor of telling everyone?" she hazarded. "Come on, I'm poking fun because you don't have anything to worry about. Amos used to be a teacher at St. Zegoba's when I was a teenager. Mr. Aposhine was always banging on about dark magic and how we had to be careful. *'Don't run in the hallways Zelda, next thing you'll turn to the dark side!' 'Make sure you hand in your homework Zelda, only a dark witch would forget!'*"

"It's true," Daphne chipped in. She'd also gone to St. Zegoba's, though she was a few years below Zelda. "I went to throw a bottle in the trash once and I missed. Just then Mr. Aposhine came around the corner and started screaming that I was set for the dark path."

"You think he was just scaring me then," I said to the pair of them.

"Yes, that's always been his style," Zelda said. She reached her hand out to pluck a cookie off the counter when Rosie slapped it away. "Hey!"

"Hey yourself. If you want a cookie you can pay for one," Rosie warned.

Zelda looked at me as though I'd back her up. "What about my sisterly privileges?"

"The privilege is that Rosie the guard dog gave you a mere slap on the wrist instead of throwing you out the back door," I joked. "Anyway, you're getting us churros on the way to the library, remember?"

"I was hoping you'd forgot about that," Zelda grumbled.

Once I had removed the buttercream from my hands, I got ready to leave and Zelda and I made our way to the library. "So," I said through a mouthful of hot churro after stopping at the cart, "Where have you been sneaking off to recently?"

"Excuse me?" Zelda said, putting on her best *I don't know what you're talking about* face.

"Come on, it's been several weeks now, and I've not said anything—none of us have actually, but we've all noticed. You've been sneaking to Wildwood, dressed in your hot country girl threads."

Zelda continued to feign ignorance. "I don't know what you're talking about."

"Really?" I said, stopping on the sidewalk and facing her. With my free hand I pulled the collar of her hoodie away from her body, revealing a pink flannel shirt. "Because you're literally wearing the outfit underneath your clothes."

She batted my hand away. "Will you stop that?!" she hissed. "How many normal people go around looking underneath their sister's clothes?"

"How many normal people have a secret outfit on underneath their clothes?" I countered.

Zelda opened her mouth to argue but then closed it again. She carried on down the sidewalk and I caught up to her. "What's with all the secrets? I thought we were done keeping secrets now? I've told you everything about me and Hudson!"

"I just have a hard time sharing private stuff, okay? Sabrina and

Celeste are wicked gossips and growing up around them would make anyone cagey about divulging personal matters."

"Well, that's fair," I said. Although I loved my cousins, they were definitely fat little grubs for the gossip vine. "I'm not like that though. Haven't we been over this before?"

"Helen says it takes several repeated instances of trust before a cycle of doubt can be broken," Zelda said as we walked up the steps to the library.

"Who is Helen?"

"She's my therapist. I've told you about her before."

I did recall Zelda mentioning a therapist before, though I don't think I'd ever had a name. "Do you think I need therapy?" I asked.

"I think everyone should try it once, but you especially."

I did a double take at that. "What's that supposed to mean?"

"Zora since moving here you've directly stumbled over, what, like four bodies?" she pointed out.

"That stuff doesn't keep me up at night though!" I paused and considered something. Was my lack of trauma normal? "Wait... *that's* why you think I need a therapist."

Zelda laughed as though I wasn't getting the point. "No, there's just a lot in there—" She jabbed her finger against my temple. "That you don't let out."

"Is not."

"Is too. For instance, every time I've tried to ask you something about your dad, you change the subject."

"That is *not* true. By the way, do you want to try and get tickets for Swan Lake this Christmas?"

"Your honor I rest my case!" Zelda said, throwing her hands up in the air for dramatic effect. "You *literally* just tried to change the subject." Zelda opened the doors for the library, and I reluctantly went inside.

"Okay, so you might have a *small* point," I conceded. To be honest I hadn't talked much about my father to anyone since he died a few years ago. "It's still raw for me I guess."

Zelda stopped in the middle of the library's empty foyer. "How about we make a deal? You tell me something about your dad, and I tell you why I'm sneaking off to Wildwood."

I stood there for a moment as I considered the proposal. "He was a huge baseball fan," I said. "He actually died in his Yankees jersey."

"How did he go?" Zelda asked sincerely.

"Heart attack. He loved his salty snacks, and he loved working in the garden. Not a good combination for a middle-aged man with a spare tire around the waist. The doctor said it was quick from the looks of things."

"I'm sorry to hear it," she said, giving me a small hug.

I pushed her away playfully. "Alright, your turn. Spit it out. Why have you been sneaking off to Wildwood?"

"I've been helping Will and Derry out on their farm. Ever since they went 'straight' they've been inundated with business, and they're struggling to keep up with demand," she answered. "I've got lots of experience working with horses, and they need employees they can trust."

"Working with your ex? How are you finding that?" I asked her. I'd only actually met Zelda's ex, Will Hackerty, recently for the first time. Zelda grew up in Wildwood, a small rural town on the west coast of the lake, with a reputation for harboring country-minded folk that liked operating outside of the law.

Will Hackerty was her childhood sweetheart and they'd even been engaged at one point, but Zelda broke off the engagement and left town several years ago after growing tired of his shortsighted criminal ways. Zelda and I were both called back to Wildwood recently to investigate a theft for Zelda's nutjob grandmother, an old hillbilly bandit by the name of Nana Bucktooth, who wanted to know who was stealing her 'Moon Juice', a magical ingredient used in potion brewing.

After some detective work we traced the stolen goods back to Will Hackerty's farm. He and Zelda's real father, a man named Billy Brewer, had stolen the Moon Juice to help nurse an injured mythical creature back to health. Apparently Will Hackerty and his brother were no longer criminals, but Will had agreed to help Billy Brewer out with this last problem to pay off an old debt.

"You know what's weird, that it doesn't actually feel all that weird? We've been getting on really well, honestly I should probably stop going over there before I start falling for him again."

"Is that a legitimate concern?" I asked her.

"I think I'll always have a small spot in my heart for him, and now that he's given up his old ways…" She shook her head and looked at me. "I left him because I was convinced he'd never stop with his petty criminal ways, but now he's actually stopped and grown up…"

"You're falling for him again."

Zelda nodded her head but sighed. "Yeah, but here's the thing. I'm an idiot."

"My darling Zelda, I already knew that," I said with a grin, placing a hand on her shoulder.

Zelda swept my arm out of the way. "Will asked me out to dinner the other night, and I panicked and told him I was seeing someone."

I stared at her. "Why on earth did you do that? You're not even in a relationship. You're so single you—actually I don't have a funny end to that thought. Just pretend I said something hilarious."

"Ha ha," she said in a robotic deadpan manner. "Anyway, I just found out that he's going out for drinks with some other girl tonight, and it's all because I lied about being with someone! He asked me first!"

"Just tell him the truth then, he'll understand."

"No, that's too easy. I have to think of something else. In fact, *you* need to help me."

"Okay, give me your phone and I'll tell him the simple truth—that you're an idiot."

"On second thought I'll figure it out on my own. Let's just go and see what's happening with the magical library."

"Who's changing the subject now?" I muttered.

Together we went over to the secret entrance to the Magical Library. In the circular foyer of the regular human library there were several display stands with information about Compass Cove's history. One particular stand covered a brief yet gruesome period in the town's history when local witches were rounded up and burned at the stake for their magical sins. I don't know who decided this stand in particular would be the secret entrance to the Magical Library, but evidently, they had a wicked sense of humor.

Zelda traced her finger around the carved wooden frame on the glass display cabinet and the magical entrance opened. The cabinet slid out of the way and revealed a spiral staircase that descended into the ground, leading to the Magical Library. There wasn't anyone else in the foyer at the moment, but if there was, they wouldn't see this magical transformation because of a wall of magic cloaking us.

As the spiral staircase revealed itself, we both spotted the note that I had seen a few weeks earlier: *Closed due to emergency, back soon. Maybe.*

"Huh, that doesn't look good," Zelda remarked.

The top of the spiral staircase was also boarded up with planks of wood that had been nailed haphazardly across the entrance. "What are we supposed to do?" I asked. "There's literally no way in!"

Zelda rolled her eyes and pulled out her wand. "If you're going to let a sign control your life, yeah, maybe." Zelda pointed the wand at the planks of wood. *"Forta deschis!"* A beam of sparkling blue light shot out from the end of her wand and hit the planks. The wood rattled slightly but nothing else happened.

"Two things surprise me here," I said. "The first is that *you* of all people are trying to break the rules, and the second is that it didn't work."

"Zora this is the library, it's basically my territory, alright? You're looking at one of Compass Cove's only members of the Emerald-level Bookworm club, so just—"

"Gold-level," I said.

"Excuse me?"

"You're in the *Gold-level* Bookworm club. You were demoted by Agnes after we snuck into the restricted section, so you're not Emerald-level anymore, you're gold. Why is emerald above gold anyway? It doesn't make any sense."

Zelda stared at me with her mouth open for a moment. "Get your wand out, you try."

"What is that going to achieve?"

"Well, your magic is a lot stronger than mine, so you can probably break through these defenses."

"You're not concerned about getting demoted to Copper-level for breaking into the library?" I asked.

She blew air through her lips. "Copper-level? Agnes would be out of her mind to try and send me all the way back down to Copper. I'd sooner tear up my library membership then fall back in the dirt with those Copper-level peasants!"

I just shook my head. "Sometimes I think I can predict what will come out of your mouth, and then you come out with madness like that."

"Can you just hurry up and try this spell already?"

With a dramatic huff I pulled out my wand and pointed it at the boards. "What's the spell again?"

"Forta deschis," she reminded me. "It's old Romany magic. It basically means 'force open'. Just say it gently, because it can be quite strong if you evoke too much."

I took a deep breathe, and with my most calming voice I said the words, *"Forta deschis."*

Now I'm happy to say that the spell *did* work, because my magic *did* remove the boards from the top of the spiral staircase.

Unfortunately, it didn't quite happen in the way I had envisioned.

As soon as I said the words a colossal beam of white light erupted from the end of my wand and a huge ball of explosive magical light sent Zelda and I hurtling across the library foyer and onto the ground. When I stood up my ears were ringing, the ground felt like it was shaking, and I felt a little dizzy.

Looking over I saw Zelda push herself onto all fours. Her face was covered in soot, and her hair was smoking.

"ARE YOU OKAY?!" I shouted, trying to hear my own voice over the ringing.

"WHAT?!" she shouted back.

"I SAID, ARE YOU—" The ringing stopped, and I realized just how loud I was shouting. "Ahem, are you okay?"

"I THINK—I think so." Zelda got to her feet, came over and helped me up too. "Flipping heck, Zora, what the deuce was that?!"

"I don't know. You heard me, I said it calmly!" I looked at my wand in disbelief and quickly put it away. No way I was using the pencil-sized nuclear bomb again anytime soon.

"You did," she agreed. "Maybe we need to work on understanding the limits of your power. It's like you're operating on a different level altogether. Hang on a second, someone's over there."

As the smoke cleared from my magical explosion, sure enough I saw the silhouette of a small figure standing by the hidden magical entrance. They couldn't be much taller than four feet, a bald impish figure with bright red skin and pointed ears, wearing a very expensive looking suit.

"Alright," the imp said in a strong Italian accent. "Which idiot is responsible for blowing the hole in the floor?"

"That would be me," I responded.

"Okay, you've got our attention. Come with me. You get five minutes with the boss."

"The boss?" Zelda asked.

"Did I stutter?" the imp said, chewing at a toothpick in his mouth. "You've got five minutes. You want them or not?"

Zelda and I looked at one another. "I guess so," I said, wondering what we were getting ourselves into now.

It looked like we were about to find out.

CHAPTER 3

"So I guess you broads is witches, huh?" the imp said as we followed him down the staircase.

"Broads? Little old-fashioned, don't you think?" I asked. Even though I was talking to a three-foot tall magical creature with bright red skin, I wasn't going to give him a free pass for casual sexism.

"Eh, cheer up darling, you'd look prettier if you smiled!" the imp said with a little cackle. He glanced back to see my disapproving glare and rolled his eyes. "Oh, relax already, it was just a joke. I might look mischievous, but I assure you I'm 'woke' too. I think all humans are equally stupid, regardless of what's between their legs."

"You were *almost* there," Zelda muttered.

"Can you tell us what's going on here?" I asked the imp. "What are you? Some sort of mafiosi imp?"

The imp suddenly stopped and turned on the spiral staircase, meaning that Zelda and I had to stop abruptly too. "First of all, *imp* is seen as a racial slur these days, so if you're going to lecture me about not being woke enough then you should educate yourself, cupcake."

"I'm sorry—" I began to stammer, but the imp burst out laughing in my face.

"Nah, I'm just kidding!" he wailed in his gravelly Italian accent.

"Yeah of course I'm an imp. But if you're suggesting I'm involved with some sort of organized crime outfit because I like to wear fine Italian suits… then you'd be two for two."

"I thought imps were from the underworld," Zelda said.

"…Yes?" the imp said, as though he was waiting for her to say something else.

"It's just… you're obviously from Italy. So, what's that about?"

"We lived in Italy for a few centuries, and now—we're here! Now hurry up, Big Tony is a busy man!" The imp resumed walking down the staircase and we followed him. After another minute we reached the bottom and stepped into the huge sprawling space that was the magical library.

It was a gargantuan room with a monolithic domed ceiling. Just ahead of us was the circular central desk. Stemming out from the desk like spokes on a wheel were vast bookcases with hundreds and hundreds of shelves. Each shelf was easily the height of a two-story house, and they stretched into the distance without an apparent end.

The library looked very much the same as it had last time I'd been here, but this time there was one marked difference: hundreds of little, red-skinned imps walking around in designer Italian suits, carrying piles of books in their arms.

"Hey Tony!" a passing imp said to our escorting imp.

"Hey Tony, how you doing?" our imp responded.

Another passing imp addressed our imp. "Tony! Poker tonight?"

"No can do, Tony, I've got to do that thing with Tony."

"Tell him that Tony still wants that money!"

"Yeah, yeah," our imp said dismissively. He turned and looked at us. "Come on, hurry up and follow me."

"I'm sorry," Zelda said as we followed the imp past the circular desk and down an avenue of books. "Are you *all* called Tony?"

"You make it sound like it's a strange thing," the imp noted.

"Well yeah… how do you differentiate?" Zelda pointed out.

"I don't know, we've had no trouble figuring it out so far." The imp lifted his head and nodded at an imp pulling books off a shelf. "Hey Tony, how's it going?"

"Not bad Tony, not bad," the other imp responded. "Hey, can you tell Tony I need that thing? What's with the broads?" it said, looking at us.

"Taking them to see Big Tony. Caught them trying to break in."

"Ooh," the other imp chuckled. "You're in trouble now!"

"How about shut up?" I said. Childish? Yeah. Hilarious? Also, yeah.

"Hey, be nice to Tony," our escorting imp said as we carried on out of earshot. "He's a good imp. Good guy."

"Which Tony are you talking about again?" I jested.

"Yeah, keep joking numb nuts. We imps don't really do names, that's more of a dumb human thing. We found one name, we like it, so we're all Tony. Keep making fun, your culturally insensitive ways don't bother me."

"I'm not culturally insensitive!" I said defensively.

"Stop making fun of our ways then, just because we're different, doesn't mean we're wrong, capeesh?"

"He's got a point Zora," Zelda said.

"Who's side are you on?!" I shouted.

After a few minutes of walking, we arrived at an improvised structure that had been assembled from books. It resembled a crude castle and was quite impressive from its sheer size. "What the heck is this?" Zelda muttered under her breath.

We approached a set of double-doors guarded by two more imps wearing black sunshades. "What have we've got here, Tony?" one of the guard imps said to our escort.

"Hey Tony, I caught these two Tonys trying to break in upstairs, I'm taking them to see Big Tony."

"Hold on a second," Zelda said. "*Our* names aren't Tony!"

"Yeah," I added, "that's actually quite culturally insensitive to assume so."

The imp rolled his eyes, put fingers to the bridge of his nose and sighed. "In the name of Big Tony, you might be the most annoying humans I ever met. What are your stupid names then?"

"I'm Zelda, and this is Zora," Zelda said.

The imp screwed up its little face. "Seriously? You're going to stand there and lecture me about us all having the same name, and your names sound exactly the same?"

"I guess they are kind of similar..." I conceded.

"Look, up there you're both called whatever you want, but down here in Big Tony's den, your both Tonys? Capeesh?"

"Why do you keep saying capeesh?" Zelda asked.

The imp didn't even respond, he just turned back around and faced the guards again. "Give me strength Tony."

The guards opened the doors and motioned the imp to go through. Zelda and I followed, crouching as we walked through the makeshift double-doors. We followed Tony down waist-high corridors, every surface made from books that had been placed together, seemingly by magic.

"Who made this thing?" I asked.

"We did," the imp answered. "We imps our builders. That's what we do by nature. You need a roof fixing or some decking putting down, let me know, my cousin is a dab hand at that sort of thing."

"I think I know him actually, it's Tony, right?" Zelda joked.

The imp looked back at Zelda, seemingly unimpressed. "Keep joking, Tony, keep joking!"

At the end of the corridor another pair of imp guards waved us through more doors, and at the heart of the structure there was a large room, in the middle of which was a big imp, similar in size to an elephant. He looked like the other smaller imps, but he had long curling horns and obviously was markedly different in size. He too was wearing a fancy-looking Italian suit.

'Big Tony' was sitting on a throne made from books. A constant stream of imps came through the room, each one setting down a pile of books at Big Tony's feet before they moved on again. As we walked over to him, I saw the large imp pick up books and drop them into his mouth, over and over again, like a constant buffet.

"Well, what do we have here?" the large imp boss said in a booming Italian voice as we approached. "Tony? I thought you were supposed to be watching the staircase."

"I was boss, and then Tony and Tony here came along and blasted it wide open with magic. These broads is witches."

"Witches, eh?" Big Tony said as he dropped a couple more books into his mouth and chewed on them. He sucked at his barstool-sized fingertips as though he'd just finished a plate of wings and sat up in his chair, pulling out a cigar that was easily the size of a bed. He lit it and puffed out a giant plume of smoke. "So, why is a couple of Tony witches breaking into the domain of Big Tony?"

"First of all, this is Compass Cove Magical Library," I said. "Or it was a few weeks ago at the very least."

Big Tony guffawed and chewed on his cigar. "Yeah, not anymore Tony, this is mine now. All these books you see? They belong to me. Now tell me what you want before I condemn you to the eternal fires of suffering."

I looked at Zelda, sensing this wasn't going to be easy. "This is *our* library," I repeated. "What we want is to know why you're here, and why you think you can just take over and act like you've always been here?"

"And how to get you out," Zelda added quietly.

"I'm here because I'm a knowledge demon, and this here library has an almost infinite supply of books for me to devour." With that admission Big Tony picked up another stack of books and dropped them into his mouth. "These here are my minions; they bring me my books. I see you've already met Tony there," he said, nodding to our escort.

"Yes, quite the diverse cast of employees you have," I murmured. "Listen, we just want our library back, and we also want to know what you did with the witches that worked here."

"They're safe and sound," Big Tony said. "Frozen in demonite. I can unfreeze them at any time." Big Tony thumbed to the wall behind us. I hadn't noticed on the way in, but there were half a dozen statues, which I now realized were the former staff members of the library.

"Statues!" I gasped. "You can't just turn people into statues!"

"Relax," our imp escort said. "It's demonite. Completely harmless and reversible. I can get you a good deal if you're intere—"

"I froze them for interrupting my meal," Big Tony said, an edge of irritability becoming apparent in his voice. "And I'm going to freeze both of you too, if you take up much more of my time. Are we done here?"

"No," I said, unperturbed by the large demon's threats. "How do we get you out of here, and how do we get our library and friends back?"

Big Tony just cackled some more. "Hm, let me see, Tony, how long did it take us to finish that witch library under Rome?" he said to a passing imp.

"Sheesh, I think it was 200 years boss? Not long, that's for sure," the imp dumped more books at his boss's feet and carried on out of the room.

"There you have it. Two hundred years or so and I should be finished in here, then we'll find another witch library. Don't worry, once I'm done, we don't hang around long. You can have your room and friends back then."

"We'll all be dead in two hundred years," I pointed out. "Humans don't live that long."

Big Tony shrugged. "That doesn't really sound like my problem, cupcake. Now get out, I think we're done here, unless you can find something more appetizing than an almost infinite library."

"Uh..." I said as I drew a long blank.

"That's what I thought. Now get out of here before I add a couple more statues to my collection."

With that our escort imp walked us back through the library, all the way to the spiral staircase again. "Look, don't take it personally, but a knowledge demon like Big Tony needs to consume a couple thousand books a day, and witch libraries just happen to be pretty large. Once we're done here, we'll be out of your hair! You broads is annoying, but you seem like a couple of good Tonys. Just stay out of Big Tony's way and we won't have any problems!"

"Unfortunately, I don't think that's going to work for us," I said as we reached the top of the staircase. "We'll think of something. One thing is for sure, we're getting this library back."

Tony laughed lightly. "Hey, if you say so doll face. Now you have a good day now, and don't be blasting any more holes in Big Tony's den, he won't be so forgiving next time, capeesh?"

The little imp disappeared back into the spiral staircase and the nailed planks magically repaired themselves, closing the entrance up once more. Zelda and I left the library and stepped outside into the fresh air, considering the pleasant spring morning.

"Zora, you heard that big guy back there, how on earth do we convince him to leave?" Zelda asked me.

"I don't know yet Zelda, but I'm sure I'll think of something."

All I had to do was find something that appeased the seemingly endless appetite of a greedy knowledge demon.

Just another normal day in Compass Cove.

CHAPTER 4

The next day I was walking through the park, talking on my phone with my boyfriend, Hudson. "Can't you do anything though? I thought a book-eating demon would fall right under the jurisdiction of MAGE."

"This Big Tony is a knowledge demon, right?" Hudson asked as manner of clarification.

"Yeah, he's huge, and he eats like a thousand books a day or something."

Hudson made a sound as though he understood. "Listen, I've heard about these guys before, but there are some things that MAGE won't touch, and that's one of them."

My boyfriend Hudson worked for a secret magical organization called MAGE, which stood for, *Magical Anomalies and General Enigmas*, at the moment his particular area of work involved keeping the general public safe from rogue magical creatures. Although he wasn't magical, the organization had magically enhanced Hudson with super strength and speed. I figured a library-invading demon was right up his alley.

"What?! Why on earth not?!"

"...That's a good question actually, let me look it up." A few moments of silence passed over the phone while I heard Hudson typing on a keyboard in the background. "Ah yeah, there it is."

"What is it?"

"We have history. Knowledge demons are dangerous things, Zora, and once they get in it's almost impossible to get them out again. There was an incident back in the 1970's at MAGE headquarters, a knowledge demon got in and ate through like a quarter of the secret archives."

"What are the secret archives?" I asked.

"They're like these archives, but they're secret," he said, not-so-helpfully.

"Well thanks for clearing that one up," I said sarcastically.

"I'm sorry," he said with a regretful laugh, "but you know there are things I'm not allowed to say about work. My point is that MAGE had a difficult time getting rid of their problematic knowledge demon. In the end they had to clone an entire witch library and bury it under some random desert town near a place called… Vanish Valley?"

"But how does that stop you from helping me out now?"

"Do me a favor and look at your right palm."

I stopped walking and did so. "Okay, I'm looking at my right palm, now what?"

"Is there anything unusual there? Like a red freckle?"

As I looked at my right palm sure enough, I did see a red freckle there, one that definitely hadn't been there the day before. "Yes! What does that mean?"

"It's a demon mark. Looks like you've got a little friend following you. Point your wand at the red freckle and use this spell, *Obtine Afara*."

"What does that do? I'm a little anxious about using my wand at the moment, because every spell I perform comes out at 1000%."

"It will remove whatever imp has attached itself to your body. People call them mischievous for a reason. That thing will bind itself to your aura and follow you around, looking for more libraries to consume. If I go to the Magic Library, I'll pick up an imp follower without a doubt. I can't risk taking one of those things back to MAGE HQ by accident."

Seeing as I was right by my bakery I decided to hurry back there before performing any magic. I ran straight upstairs to my apartment, closed the door behind me and pulled my wand out.

"Zora!" my familiar Hermes said from the kitchen table. "How's it going?"

"Give me a minute Hermes," I said as I pointed the wand tip at my palm. "Hudson, what was the spell again?" Hudson repeated the spell and I cast it. *"Obtine Afara!"*

Another blinding flash of white light erupted from the wand, but there was no explosion this time thankfully. Instead, a small imp shot out of my hand, collided with the ceiling and crashed to the kitchen floor. I pointed my wand at it as it stood up, rubbing its head and groaning.

"Ouch..." the imp said in its gravelly Italian accent. "Sheesh lady, was that really necessary?"

"You! You've been following me!" I gasped.

"Relax, I was just following orders! I snuck onto your hand when you were talking to Big Tony!" the stalker imp revealed.

"So you're not the staircase imp?"

"No, but if you see Tony then—"

"Get out of my apartment and tell your boss I'm coming for him!"

"Whatever you say doll face," the imp chuckled. It drew a circle of fire on the floor, jumped through and the portal closed behind it.

"You know most people just get gum stuck on their shoe," Hermes said from the kitchen table. "Walking an entire imp into the apartment? I'm impressed."

"Will you shush for a moment?" I said to Hermes. "Hudson?"

"Yeah?" he responded down the phone.

"I've got rid of it, I think. Are there any more of them?"

"Most likely it'll be just the one, but it probably won't hurt to do a full body check just in case."

"What about Zelda? She was there too?"

"Yeah, most likely she's got a tracker friend too. You'll both need complete body checkups. We've got a couple of female doctors at MAGE that could help you out... obviously you can't come here though. I'll have them come and visit you. Can Zelda be at your apartment in the next twenty minutes?"

"Let me call and check," I groaned. "I'll speak with you in a bit."

I hung up the phone and dialed Zelda's number. While waiting Hermes continued to pipe up. "Full disclosure, if there's some sort of head-to-toe body checkup happening then I don't want to be in the same room," he said.

"But who will provide the asinine commentary?" I asked. Before he could respond Zelda answered the phone.

"I *just* got finished with the morning shift at the café, whatever you need help with, it can wait, I'm going home for a bath," Zelda said.

"Hello to you too. I've got bad news for you; you need to come over to my apartment." I explained to her about the demon mark, and she sounded suitably freaked out.

"These things are on us? What? Gross!"

"Just get over here, Hudson is sending someone to help sort it out."

Not long after that Zelda arrived at my apartment, and a few minutes after that Hudson's friend from the agency arrived too. I answered the door and was surprised to see a woman standing there in a complete hazmat suit.

"Can't be too careful," she said with a jovial laugh, the sound coming from a speaker on her waist. "Who wants to go first?"

I'm not sure if the word 'embarrassed' quite covers it, but the next twenty minutes was equally mortifying for both Zelda and I. Monica, Hudson's friend in the hazmat suit, did individual inspections of us both. There were no more marks on me, but there was one on Zelda, on the heel of her right foot.

"Nothing personal, just business!" the discovered imp shouted as it jumped through a portal ring of fire and disappeared.

Once Monica was suitably satisfied that Zelda and I no longer had any imps hitching a ride on our auras, she removed the visor on her hazmat suit and set it down on the table. "From now on you can use this to see if you've got any more unwanted visitors." Monica pulled out two small devices not much bigger than a key fob and handed them to us. The little fobs looked like little white skulls. "It won't be as easy for a spirit to hide on your body now, so just run this little scanner over yourself if you want to make sure, and it'll tell you if anything is present. I've got a demo…"

Monica pulled out a little glass box from her satchel. Inside there was some sort of scaly looking monkey. "This is an envy imp, and if I run the scanner over it…" Monica moved the little skull fob over the box and sure enough it reacted. The eyes lit up red and the mouth started moving.

"Demon! Demon alert!" the skull fob said.

"Simple as that," Monica grinned. She swished the fob over both of us again quickly and there was no result. "There you go. All good! Nice meeting y'all!"

Once Monica was gone Zelda grumbled something about 'hating magic' and went home to have her bath. I texted Hudson to let him know the problem was resolved and thanked him for the heads up about the demon mark.

"Knowledge demon, eh?" Hermes said. "They don't crop up too often. Not heard anything about them for a few hundred years. Once they find a place they're usually preoccupied for a while."

"How do I get rid of it?" I asked. "There must be something I can do."

"First port of call is contact the Compass Cove Magic Council and let them know that the Magic Library is done-zo," he said.

"Are you kidding me? That's not helping anyone."

"I'm not kidding. Once a knowledge demon gets hold of a library that's it. The standard protocol is to start building a new library."

"But there are people in there! That demon turned them into statues!"

"Hm… not ideal. We'll have to make some sort of deal with him to get the people unfrozen. What did they use?"

"They said something about demonite, I think."

"Demonite! Heh, that stuff is fantastic. I could really do with getting some for the magic pantry actually—"

"Hermes!"

"Okay, okay, easy! I'll contact the Magic Council and let them know about the library. They probably already know to be honest. I wonder what the new library will look like..."

"I wonder if Fancy Bill will be able to help me with this?" I asked.

I went back downstairs to the bakery pantry, which was the temporary home for Fancy Bill. As a talking skull with flaming blue eyes, he was a little unsettling to say the least, so I put him somewhere he would be relatively out of sight.

"Well look who came crawling back," Fancy Bill sang as I came into the pantry.

"I need your help."

"Better late than never. What do you want?"

"If I ask you to research knowledge demons, how long do you think you'll be asleep?" Fancy Bill was an *Oracle*, a rare magical... *thing* that had access to all the knowledge in the universe but had to go into a long meditative trance to sort through that information for relevant answers.

"I'm not going to beat around the bush, Zora, knowledge demons aren't dime a dozen. I could bite the bullet and look it into it for you, but I'd probably be as useful as a chocolate teapot—"

"Can you just stop talking in idioms for one minute and give me a straight answer?"

"Me-ow, this cat's got claws! If you didn't want me to speak in idioms, you shouldn't have sent me researching them!" Fancy Bill said, his flaming blue eyes flickering away vacantly.

"Do me a favor, forget everything you know about idioms and tell me about knowledge demons. How do I get one out of a library?"

"Pah, I don't have to go into a trance to give you that answer. It's very easy."

My hopes suddenly lifted. "It is? What do I do?"

"Wait about two hundred years until the demon has finished eating all the books, then ta-da! The library is yours again. That is the only known solution for removing a knowledge demon from a library."

I stared at Fancy Bill for a moment with my mouth hanging open. "Are you actually kidding me? That can't be the only way. I mean it's as simple as getting a thing out of another thing. It's not rocket science, is it?"

"What's that supposed to mean?" Fancy Bill asked. "Who said anything about rocket science?"

"It's an expression, you bone-headed idiot, I thought you of all... *things* would know that."

"You just told me to forget everything I know about idioms, so I did."

I had to admit he had me there. "You know you might be the most useless all-knowing being in the universe?"

"I could look into that for you if you'd like?" Fancy Bill suggested.

"I'm leaving now, before I pull my hair out."

"Have a nice day!" he sarcastically called as I left the pantry.

CHAPTER 5

Despite having a constant stream of problems to deal with in Compass Cove, the bakery was still one of my main priorities. Thankfully I had Rosie and Daphne to help hold the fort now, which meant I could spend more time out and about in town whenever my services were needed, but I still spent a lot of my time in the shop making sure the business was running smoothly.

The next morning started normally enough, the three of us were in the bakery bright and early to get the morning bake done, and by the time the sun had come up and the rest of Compass Cove was awake, our wares were fully stocked and flying off the shelves as a steady stream of customers came through the door.

After the morning rush hour was done things quietened down a little bit and we had a moment to have a breather. At this point we usually took a break and had a nice drink and a chat while attending to the odd customer as they came into the shop. I'd say about eighty percent of our daily business happened around opening and around lunch. Around those busy periods things were pretty chill, so there was plenty of opportunity for the three of us to socialize.

"Of course, he wasn't too happy after I threw him in the river," Rosie said, reaching the end of another one of her insane stories. "But what did he expect was going to happen? Anyway, the gendarme said they didn't want to see me back in Paris. Apparently, they frown upon foreigners throwing the mayor into the water."

Daphne and I just stared at her in amazement. If it was anyone else, I'd suspect half of these stories were made up, but Rosie might just be the most interesting (and dangerous) woman in the world.

"I saw a possum in my back yard once," Daphne offered. "That's about as interesting as my life gets."

"I'm thinking of trying tea with two sugars..." I added. Both Daphne and Rosie looked at me and scoffed. "What?"

"Oh, come on Zora," Rosie said in her Irish lilt. "My life is tame in comparison to yours!"

Daphne nodded in agreement. "She's right, Zora. You're always getting into trouble. It basically walks through the door once a week."

"It does not!" I said, though secretly I very much agreed with that sentiment. "Come on, let's get started with tidying up the back, maybe we can close early today if all the jobs are done."

The three of us went into the back, me at the rear of the pack. A customer came through the door, so I turned on my heels and came back to the register with my best customer-facing grin.

"Good morning! How may I help you... today?" My warm enthusiasm simmered away about halfway through my greeting, as I took proper stock of the man that had just walked into my shop. He was tall, thin, with pale skin and messy dark hair. He had his hands in his pockets and walked up to the counter, his eyes barely meeting mine.

"So, you sell cakes?" he asked.

"Yes... this is a bakery. Did you want to buy something?"

The unusual stranger looked up at me, his pale green eyes making me feel slightly uneasy. "My name is Niles, I thought I should probably introduce myself."

"Um... hi," I said. "My name is Zora; this is my shop. What can I get for you Niles?"

"Blake told me to introduce myself," Niles said tonelessly. "I'm his temporary replacement."

"Excuse me?"

"He had to go away on pack business. Wolf politics, I won't bore you with the details. I'll be watching you until he gets back."

I don't know why but that made me feel quite uncomfortable. Blake was a mountain of muscle and a rather charismatic extrovert, this guy looked like he'd just walked out of rehab and came from the wrong side of the tracks. "Uh… you're a little different to Blake."

Niles nodded as though he'd heard that before. "Yes, we're not very alike, but he said I was the best man for the job, so here I am. I'm not really big on the whole 'talking' thing, so don't expect to see much of me. If I had it my way you wouldn't know I'm here at all, but Blake said I should say hello. Now that's done, so—" the mysterious Niles turned to leave when I stopped him.

"Wait a second!" I called.

Niles shuffled back around. "What?"

"How long will Blake be gone for?"

He shrugged. "I don't know. As long as it takes to get this pack politics sorted. It's usually either very fast, or very slow. It depends if anyone ends up fighting to the death."

"…Right," I said and scratched the back of my head. "Do you want a drink or something to eat?"

Niles took a quick look at the offerings on display and shook his head. "No, none of this stuff is really to my taste."

Yikes. *Tell me how you really feel.* "Okay then. Well… be seeing you around. Or not? I guess. Bye?"

"Yep," Niles said and left the shop. After he was gone Daphne came into the front, I just *knew* that she and Rosie had been listening from the back of the shop.

"Trouble right on cue then," she said with a laugh.

"Don't you start. Come on, let's get back to work."

After we got the back all tidied up things started to get busy in the shop again as lunchtime neared. When the rush passed Daphne's shift finished, Rosie and I said goodbye to her, and Rosie went into the back to start packing things up for the day.

The shop was quiet again, so I pulled out my phone and called Blake, he answered pretty much straightaway.

"Zora! Is everything okay?" he asked in alarm.

"Will you relax? I'm just calling to see how you're doing."

"Oh, I'm fine," he said, his voice calming a little. "I've been called away temporarily on pack business, I won't bore you with the details, werewolf politics are—"

"Very boring, yeah, I know, *Niles* just dropped by to tell me as much."

"Ah, so you've met then," Blake said with a little trepidation.

"If you can call that meeting someone. Who is that guy, Blake? He gives me the freaking creeps. That's seriously the person you chose as your replacement guardian?"

"It's just temporary, and I know Niles seems a little bit detached. Conversation and emotions aren't really his jam, but I swear after me he's the best in the business. I trained Niles as a guardian myself, he's the best student I ever had."

"He's also a psychopath," I noted. "It was like I was talking to a robot."

"I know he comes across like that, but trust me, Niles is a good guy —he's just been through some stuff is all."

"Right, but a big part of being a witch is following intuition, right? And the Sisters of the Shade seem to have a way past the magical boundaries guarding the town. Hudson thinks there's a traitor among us, and this Niles guy—"

"Hudson and I have talked about the traitor theory, and I think he's probably onto something, but I can assure you Niles is on our side. Trust me. Besides, this is first day in town, he's been out in the woods with my pack the rest of the time, he can't be the one messing with the boundaries," Blake pointed out.

"He could just easily mess with the boundaries from the outside, right?"

"No, whoever is doing it has to be on the inside, so—Niles is not your man. Zora, I'd hope you know me by now, do you really think I'd handpick a replacement I didn't trust with my own life?"

I sighed in acknowledgment. "You know what, you're right. I apologize. I'll give creepy Niles a chance."

"How did you know about his nickname?" Blake said.

"Lucky guess. So, how are things with the wife?"

"Uh... Lori and I are still trying to navigate the stormy waters of an arranged marriage. Right now, things are fine, but we don't really have much in common," he admitted.

"Do you guys really have to go through with it?" I asked.

"Yeah, I'm afraid we don't have much choice. Still, Lori's a fine girl, I could have been paired with worse. We'll just have to take things one day at a time. How about you? How's the love boat holding up with Hudson?"

"No complaints there. Does he know you're out of town yet? It'll tear him up."

Until very recently Hudson and Blake had pretty much been mortal enemies, but after getting stuck with a joining curse by a mad old witch they actually became pretty good friends.

"Yeah, I called him earlier, and stop making it sound like we're dependent on each other!"

"I just calls them as I sees them, friend. Alright I better go, a customer just came in."

"Alright, later Zora."

Now I will admit that my customer service skills sometimes aren't always *perfect*, but as I saw my next customer come through the door a big smile spread across my face. It was Saxophone Joe, one of my favorite regulars.

"Saxophone Joe!" I said warmly. "I was wondering where you were today. Same as usual?"

"Don't you know it, Zora," he said and came up to the counter. Joe was an older homeless man originally from New Orleans. Apparently, he moved to Compass Cove a few years and now made money by playing saxophone in the park. "I would have been in earlier, but I've just been feeling the music today, know what I mean?"

"Sometimes I get in the flow and lose track of time too. How are the tips today?"

"Not bad, not bad. I'm going to get that Ferrari any day now," Joe joked and handed over his money. I always tried to refuse it, but he'd just put it in the tip jar anyway. I got his usual order ready—coffee and a Danish—and Joe took a seat to talk while he had his food and drink. Once he was done, he brushed his hands off, stood up and grabbed his sax.

"Delicious as always Zora. I'll see you tomorrow."

"Have a good one, Joe."

As Joe went to leave a woman was coming into the bakery. He held the door open and stepped to one side to let her pass.

"Thank you," she said.

"Anything for a beautiful lady!" Joe sang as he skipped out onto the street.

The woman approached the counter and smiled at me. She really was uniquely beautiful, with long brown hair and delicate features. "Hey!" she said energetically.

"Good afternoon," I replied. "What can I get for you today?"

"I've heard a lot of good things about this place and finally have a chance to check it out. Those brownies look good. Maybe a hot chocolate too? To go."

"Coming right up," I said and got the order ready. "Do you work around here?"

"Not far actually. Just a couple of blocks over. I'm a therapist." The woman took a card out and handed it to me. "Helen, Helen Bowen."

"Actually, I might have heard of you. I think you're my sister's therapist…"

"Who's your sister?" Helen asked with a confused look.

"Zelda Wick."

A look of surprise came over the woman's face. "Oh! You must be Zora then." She then looked at the cafe and seemed more surprised. "And this must be *the* bakery! I never put two and two together!"

I chuckled. "I take it Zelda has told you quite a bit about me then."

"Rest assured it's all good, though I'm afraid I can't say much more than that. It's a pleasure to finally meet you though."

We chatted a little, I handed Helen her order and we said our goodbyes. Once she was gone, I went into the back and helped Rosie with the remainder of the tidying up. After Helen only a handful of people came into the shop before I decided to call it quits and closed for the day.

When Rosie left, I went up to the apartment and started running a bath. I'd just turned the faucet off when the ghost of my Aunt Constance popped her head through the wall.

"Boo!" she shrieked, her latest attempt to try and scare me.

"Good evening, Constance," I said, unphased by her latest scare attempt. "What did we say about appearing in bathrooms?"

"Something about *keep on doing it*, or *you're not nearly doing it enough*." I gave her a look. "Oh, lighten up! I just came to see how your day was."

"Surprisingly tame. No doubt you're about to turn that all upside down however."

Constance cackled. "Darling, you make me sound like a right old inconvenience. Things would be a lot more boring without me."

"Some people might use the word *peaceful*. How are the ghosts of Compass Cove anyway?"

"Don't get me started," she said and rolled her eyes. "You think I'm a handful? It's like high school never ended out there. The dead are more dramatic than the living! I think something goes in the brain once we die, because they're all stark raving mad."

"Must be difficult with you being so well adjusted," I snarked.

"You don't know the half of it, Zora," Constance said, completely missing my jibe. "Enough about me though, I want to hear about you. What crazy business do you find yourself in the middle of at the moment?"

"Actually, things have been quiet for a few weeks now. I did want to ask you something though, about the magical boundaries surrounding the town. Do you know much about them?"

Constance tilted her head. "A little, what did you want to know?"

"The Sisters of the Shade keep slipping through the boundaries somehow. They're flooding the town with cursed jewelry, and we've had several eyewitness accounts of them being in town. Aren't the boundaries supposed to keep them out?"

"Yes, that's right." Constance nodded. "Most dark witches will struggle to get into the town. If they're getting through then it suggests they have found a way, but…"

"But what?"

"Don't take this the wrong way, but you're one of their main interests, are you not? They want to recruit you because your power has far more potential than most."

"That seems to be right, yes," I said.

"Well, if they *can* get into town, wouldn't they have made another attack on you already? That's what I would do if I was a dark witch." She then added. "Speaking hypothetically of course."

"*Of course.* We think there's a traitor, someone messing with the boundaries. Would you be able to have a word with your ghost friends and maybe set up some sort of watch?" I asked.

"I can try, but you're asking a lot. People think just because we're dead us ghosts don't have much to do, but it's quite the opposite actually. I'm run off my feet with everything I have to do!"

I just stared at her. "What on earth do you have to do?"

Constance acted like she hadn't heard me. "I beg your pardon?"

"What could you have to do that keeps you so busy? You spend all day doing whatever you like."

Then she acted like she'd heard something in the next room. "Did you hear that? I think Hermes is calling me. I'll just go and see what he needs." With that Constance floated out of the bathroom, expertly avoiding the need to answer my question.

As I got into the bath and let go of the day's stresses I sank into the water and let out a long breath. I then got a funny feeling on the back of my neck, like something was about to come along and interfere with everything all over again.

It was then that my phone started ringing. I'd placed it on a stool next to the tub. Drying my hands off on a towel I leaned over and looked at the screen, sighing as I saw the caller ID on the screen: Compass Cove Police Station.

"Here we go," I muttered, and picked up the phone to answer it. "Hello?"

"Zora?" Sheriff Burt asked down the line.

"The one and only. I'm guessing this isn't a social call."

"Any chance you'd be interested in helping us out with another case? Only Blake is away on business and the rest of us…" He lowered his voice. "Well, we're a bit useless at the detective stuff."

"What's happened now?" I asked.

"Another murder. Young woman, found dead outside her office just an hour ago. Would you believe it, she was a therapist."

My heart stopped in my chest all of a sudden and I sat up in the tub. "What was her name?"

"Bowen, Helen Bowen."

"…Send me the address Burt, I'll come right on over."

CHAPTER 6

⚛

I quickly got out of the bath and headed to my bedroom to dry and get ready. Upon picking out an outfit I realized a miniature disaster was lurking: I had no clean clothes left to wear. One of the hazards of working in a bakery—even with an apron—is that one tended to get all sorts on themselves, meaning that clothes very rarely lasted more than a day.

Doing laundry was actually on my to-do list for the evening, I just hadn't anticipated I would get called out of the house tonight, so I was caught short.

It then occurred to me that I had magic at my disposal now. It was funny, even though I'd been a witch for about a couple of months I routinely forgot magic was something I had access too. I hurried across the room to my dresser and picked up *Blundell's Bumper Book of Beginner Spells*. In the index I found one spell for clothes and flicked to the corresponding page.

The Dressing Spell

Ever find yourself in a bind at the last minute? Need that perfect outfit? Have no fear, Blundell is here! Clothing spells often have an infa-

mous reputation for never working all that well, but with Blundell's breathtaking bag of brilliance, you'll never need another clothing spell again! Facing a mirror, ready your wand and state the incantation: *Vrazti pe mak!*

Note: It is very important to hold two words in your mind that suitably describe the desired outfit. For example: smart, casual. Outdoors, green.

"Okay, let's see how badly this goes," I said. I went over to full-length mirror in the corner of my bedroom, produced my wand and repeated the incantation, *"Vrazti pe mak!"* As I did this, I had two words in my head: witch, detective.

The spell took effect as an abrupt gust of glittering blue wind that thundered up from the floor, moving around my body in a corkscrew motion. It momentarily obscured my reflection, and once I could see myself again, I was wearing an English policeman's uniform, with a tall black witch hat on my head.

"Why on earth did I think this would work?" I groaned. I then heard cackling from the main apartment, I ran out of the room to see what was going on and saw the most amusing sight.

"Oh, the little hat!" Constance said with glee as she pointed as Hermes. It seemed my spell hadn't only targeted me, but Constance, Hermes, and Phoebe as well. The ghostly blue apparition of my Aunt Constance was wearing a matching outfit to me, and Phoebe the owl and Hermes the cat had on adorably cute versions as well. Phoebe was still asleep and hadn't noticed, Hermes was looking at himself in the mirror, turning his head from side to side.

"You know what, I don't hate it," he said, admiring his reflection.

"What on earth are you doing in there?" Constance asked me.

"Trying to magic up myself an outfit, all my clothes are in the laundry, and I've just been called out on a new case. I'll just have to throw on something covered in flour and get out the door quickly."

"Nonsense, use my wardrobe! I already told you the password. There's bound to be something in there!"

"Constance was something of a shopaholic in her living years,"

Hermes added, still admiring his reflection. "I doubt she's ever even worn half of that stuff."

I had sort of forgotten about Constance's magic wardrobe. "Okay thanks, I'll take a look."

"The password is *'Bungalow!'*" Constance reminded me as I walked in the direction of her room.

Constance's room was a weird shrine to Donny Osmond, every wall and surface—even the ceiling—covered in framed portraits of his freakishly large grin. I kept my eyes down and went over to the old wardrobe in the corner. As I got closer a wooden face animated on the doors.

"Password?" the wardrobe asked in its stately feminine voice.

"Bungalow."

The doors opened, revealing a set of stairs going down to… somewhere. "And what are we after today?"

"I want to look like a smart detective. Do you have something for that?"

"Is this going to be a regular thing?"

"Excuse me?"

"Coming here and asking me for clothes," the wardrobe said. "This is the second time in a month now."

"Constance said it would be okay…" I said slowly, wondering why I had to explain myself to a talking wardrobe.

"Oh, it's all very well and good for Constance, she's dead. Floating around and shrieking at all hours without a care in the world, but what about those of us left behind? Left and forgotten!" the wardrobe said dramatically.

Sighing to myself, I pushed the fingers against the bridge of my nose. "Is there something I can help you with?"

"Well, it's very good of you to ask, as a matter of fact there is. You're very perceptive."

"Hm. So what do you want?"

"Moths," the wardrobe said.

"Moths?"

"Yes, moths. I can't get rid of the darned things. It's been over two years since Constance put a mothball in here. Do you want these clothes to get eaten to bits?"

"...That's all that you want? A mothball?"

"Yes, and maybe a new coat of varnish too. But get a professional to do it, you look like the type that watches one video and thinks they know everything about furniture restoration. No offense."

"Quite accurate actually. So that's it? Mothballs and some new varnish? And you'll stop complaining?"

"Less of the attitude! It's not easy being a magic wardrobe you know! There are over forty thousand garments in here and I have to adjust them on the fly every time you—oh great and wise master—comes to my doors and starts making your daily demands!"

Man, this magic wardrobe liked to play the victim. "Again, this is only the second time I've asked you for an outfit, and after all this grief I won't come back much. My non-magic wardrobe does a very good job of giving me my clothes without insulting me."

"Darling the outfits you pick, you're insulting yourself," the wardrobe replied in its haughty manner. I just found myself staring at the piece of furniture for a few long seconds.

"How about I pick you out a nice date with a woodchipper?" I said.

The wardrobe laughed nervously. "Now, now! Just joking around! We're all friends here, no need for idle threats! Come inside and see what I have on display!"

"Can't you just throw an outfit at me like last time?" I asked warily.

"No, I insist! Only the star treatment from now on. Come on in, Zebra!"

"...My name is *Zora*. Zebras are an animal."

"You meat organisms all look the same to me, darling. Now come on in."

With a hesitant sigh I stepped inside the wardrobe and followed the dark staircase down into the unknown depths. Every surface was covered in patchwork fabric, the air smelled musty, and it was very quiet.

The patchwork staircase ended and opened into a large dim room that was honestly the size of a church. Everywhere I looked I saw an endless ocean of clothing rails and outfits. "How in the holy heck…" I muttered to myself.

"Glorious, isn't it?!" the wardrobe said, its voice echoing all around me. "This is just the main room of course. The 8:32 to party wear is coming on through now, or you can take the C-line to retro attire."

I was about to open my mouth to ask just what the wardrobe was talking about, when I turned and saw an entire train platform made out of patchwork fabric. A quilted train roared onto the platform, opened its doors and took off again a moment later.

"Just how big is this place?" I asked the wardrobe.

"Constance was afraid of running out of space, so she purchased the large magic wardrobe. Now, what kind of outfit did you want again?"

It was only then that I even remembered why I was down here. "Crikey, I really should get a move on." It had now been fifteen minutes since Burt's call, and I was still dilly-dallying around, looking for something to wear. "I just want to look smart at a crime scene. Is that too much to ask?"

"Say no more darling, I've got *just* the thing."

For a moment I stood there wondering what the wardrobe would rustle up, and then I heard the rustle of rapidly approaching fabric. I threw my hands up and screamed, "No!" as I saw the outfit hurtling towards me at the last second.

The clothes snapped around my body in a violent battle, comprised of them trying to force themselves onto me, and me trying to fight them off—unsuccessfully. Once the brief assault was over, I stood up and saw a mirror floating in front of me. "Okay… I actually look killer," I said in surprise.

"Perfect for a crime scene then," the wardrobe quipped.

She'd picked me out a pair of smart jeans, a blazer, heels, and a cute blue blouse. "I love it, but is there anything you can do about my hair?" I asked. It had gotten a little messy in the clothes attack.

"Darling I'm a magic wardrobe, not a miracle worker. But I suppose I could send a bit of wind your way…" Before I could object it felt like someone had placed an old-timey hair drying helmet on my head. After a few seconds the wind stopped and looking in the mirror I saw that my unmanageable brunette locks had been curled quite nicely.

"I think we just became best friends," I said to the wardrobe while I admired my reflection.

"Yes, yes," it replied in a bored manner. "Mothballs and varnish. Don't forget now!"

I exited the wardrobe and quickly made my way to the front door.

"Yowza!" Hermes said upon seeing me. "Dressed to kill, Zora!"

"Looks like wardrobe hasn't lost her touch yet," Constance remarked. "You look fabulous, Z. Want me to tagalong for some company? Maybe you could pick my brain if you get stuck?"

"Uh... no thanks, but you'll be the first person I come to. Try not to burn down the apartment while I'm gone."

"No guarantees!" Hermes called after me.

I hurried down the stairs and to the van in the rear parking lot. As I started the engine, I called Hudson.

"Hey," he answered. "Is everything okay?"

"Burt just called me." After a pause I added. "Well, about twenty minutes ago. There's a new case. Want to come and help me out?"

"Sure. Pick me up in five?" he asked.

"I'll be there."

* * *

"Are we heading to a crime scene or to a date?" Hudson asked with a smile as he got into the van. He leaned over and kissed me on the cheek. "You look amazing!"

"Thanks, I had some help from Constance's magic wardrobe. The rest of my clothes are covered in flour and various other ingredients. How's your day been?"

Hudson put on his seatbelt, and I started driving in the direction of our crime scene. "Not great," he said wearily. "I've been out in Fog Death Forest today actually. A group of human hikers went missing up there and I had to find them."

A chill came over me as Hudson mentioned Fog Death Forest. The dark magical forest was about twenty minutes outside of town, and it was a magical boiling pot for all sorts of dangerous entities and creatures. We'd ventured there recently to find a group of dryads—tree people—in order to get wood for my replacement wand.

"I thought humans weren't able to notice the forest?" I asked. The forest was such a dangerous area of magical mayhem that boundaries had been set up around it so that humans would drive by without stopping there.

"They're not supposed to. Someone's destroyed the magical barriers around part of the forest and of course a group of humans wandered right on in. Luckily, we got an alert on our systems and I went in after them."

"Were they okay?" I asked as I turned off the main street.

"Yeah, just about. They'd been led astray by a Fae energy. They're nasty little spirits that trick people into following them until they vanish into the thin air. The hikers thought they'd been gone for a few hours—it had been days! Fae have a way of warping time like that."

A cold shiver came over me. "Sounds creepy."

"You don't know the half of it. Anyway, the humans are okay, I blanked their memories and sent them on their way. I restored the boundary too. I'm not sure what tampered with it, but it looks like something literally ate the part of the energy boundary that was missing."

"Something *ate* the boundary?" I asked him with a querying brow.

He nodded. "That's right. I've been looking it up and it looks like there's only one creature that can eat raw magical energy like that." Hudson pulled out his phone and showed me an illustration of a magical creature that looked like someone had put the head of a pelican on the body of a goat and dipped it in canary yellow paint.

"Oh my," I said with a note of revulsion. "What the heck is that?"

"It's called a Ptera, there aren't many of them around and they're not native to these parts. You don't happen to know someone that might have one?" he asked as an afterthought.

I laughed at the absurdity of the question. "No, but I'll keep an eye out. I guess the person that keeps letting the Sisters of the Shade into town will have one of these animals then?"

Hudson shrugged and put the phone away. "At the moment I have absolutely no idea, it's the only lead we have—and I don't like how vague it is. What's the case anyway?"

"Helen Bowen," I said. "She's a therapist. I met her for the first time today actually. She's Zelda's shrink, would you believe it?"

"Does Zelda know yet?"

I shook my head. "No, and I have no idea how I'm going to break it to her."

We pulled onto the street where Helen's office was located and I parked the van. Hudson and I climbed out and made our way to the building's front doors, where Sheriff Burt's sons, Wayne and Zayne, were keeping watch.

"Evening Zora," Wayne yawned, stepping aside to let us in. "They're upstairs, Tamara's already here."

I thanked Wayne, and Hudson and I went inside and upstairs. As we climbed, I heard Sheriff Burt and Tamara Banana, the town's only CSI, talking as we approached.

"What if an owl got in here?" Burt proffered. "It could have dropped the thing on her and—"

A loud sigh followed from Tamara. "Again, I don't think an owl, an eagle, a hawk, or *any* type of bird flew in here and killed this woman," Tamara said with the frustration of a woman nearing her limit.

"Probably not, still… worth considering though."

Hudson and I came around the corner and saw the crime scene. An open door crisscrossed with police tape framed a medium-sized office, where the body of Helen Bowen lay slumped across the floor.

CHAPTER 7

"Good evening," I said, Hudson and I hovering outside the door. Burt and Tamara turned to regard us. Tamara was crouching down over the body, doing her work, while Burt provided his helpful commentary from the rear.

"Is it? Is it though?" Tamara asked me, taking a sip of a coffee. "Because I *was* cozied up in bed, enjoying a superhero movie marathon, and now I'm here, working a crime scene and fielding questions about birds."

"I'm just saying an owl might have done it," Burt reiterated to Hudson and me. "I saw this documentary once where—"

"An owl didn't do it!" Tamara said shrilly.

Just then Burt's radio crackled and one of his son's voices came through. "Dad? Mom just called through from the station. We've got reports of a vagrant sleeping rough in the park. An anonymous caller said they spotted expensive looking jewelry, looked stolen."

Burt sighed and held up his radio. "Alright, we'll go check it out now." He tucked his radio back into his belt and looked at me. "Well Wick, what do you think?"

"I think I literally just got here and don't have any facts," I said, yawning myself.

"Before I forget." Burt pulled a folded-up piece of paper out of his pocket and handed it to me. "That's a check for your work on the dead rockstar case. As you didn't respond to my requests about billing, I used a typical day rate for outside consultants and multiplied it across a week."

I unfolded the check and my eyes widened at the amount Burt had written down. "Uh, very generous of you Burt, thanks." My attention then moved to *whom* the check was made out to. "Bread Herring Inc?" I asked in a confused manner.

Burt chuckled. "I thought you might like that. The tax works out better for you if I write the check to a corporation, so I made one up. You're a baker and you're also a dab hand at solving mysteries, so I thought you'd like the pun."

"I like it," Hudson said with a grin.

"I don't have a business though… not one for mystery consultancy anyway."

"Maybe it's time you made one then," Burt suggested. "Unless you want to get taxed through the nose! Change the information on the check if you wish, now if you'll excuse me, I need to go and check out this call."

Burt left the room; I tucked the check into my pocket and ducked through the police tape. "So, what do we have here, Tamara?"

"Helen Bowen, 38, a therapist. Killed by a blow to the head. Found by the building secretary, no sign of the killer." Tamara pointed at the impact on the left temple. "Murder weapon dropped at the scene, one… chisel? I guess?" Tamara held up an evidence baggy, inside which was a heavy-looking metal chisel with a wide flat wedge and a short handle.

"Huh," I said, looking at the murder weapon.

"Not the sort of thing one would expect to find lying around in a therapist's office," Hudson remarked.

"Meaning the murderer brought it with them," Tamara said.

"*And* left it here…" I remarked. "What else do we have?"

"As for the actual scene, not much else. There was only one other person in the building at the time and that was the secretary. There does seem to be a trace of some sort of pollen on the chisel, though I'm not sure what it is at the moment. I can run a test on it, but not until I get back to the lab."

"Where's the secretary now?" Hudson asked.

"She's down at the station giving her account."

I looked at Hudson. "We should head down there and talk to her while we can."

He nodded. "Want to take a quick look around first?"

We had a quick look around the room, but I saw nothing unusual, and my intuition wasn't moving me in any particular direction. So far, we had a murder weapon and some sort of pollen—not a lot to go on.

"Did the secretary see anyone enter the building?" I asked Tamara.

She shook her head. "No, from what I gather she was in the bathroom when she heard a scream from upstairs. By the time she got up there the victim was dead on the floor and there was no sign of the assailant. She heard a car pulling away quickly outside. There are car tracks in the rear lot, though I've not had a chance to look at them yet."

"Let's check them out before we leave," Hudson said to me.

"Agreed." I looked at Tamara. "We're going to head down to the station and see what the secretary has to say. Let me know what else you find?"

"Will do," Tamara yawned. "Providing I can stay awake! The suspect left through the back fire doors from the looks of things."

"Got it, thanks," I said as we left the room.

Hudson and I went back downstairs and followed the corridor to the building's rear fire doors. They were propped open and also crossed with police tape. Out in the parking lot there were only two cars, one presumably belonging to Helen, and the other presumably belonging to the secretary, who was currently down at the police station.

We walked around to the side of the building and saw one long tire mark streaking across the asphalt. Hudson crouched down to get a better look.

"What is it?" I asked him. I knew next to nothing about cars, so a set of tread marks meant nothing to me.

"Well for one thing these marks aren't from a car tire, this is a motorbike." He stood up and pointed at the track. "Look, there's only one, and it's much too thin to be a car tire."

"So, our suspect got away on a motorbike," I said in reflection. That was significant, not a lot of people rode those things. "Alright then, let's head down to the station and see what this secretary has to say."

Hudson and I headed over to the van when a bright flash from a camera blinded us. "Hey!" Hudson yelled, holding his hand over his eyes. "Quit it with the photography!"

"Sorry!" a nasal new jersey voice responded. The camera lowered, revealing a disheveled looking man in an ill-fitting brown suit.

"Hold on a second, I recognize you, you're that sleazeball public defender that was assigned to me that one time," I said. A few months ago, I'd inadvertently become a suspect in a murder case, and as I didn't have a lawyer the police had provided me with this less than stellar specimen.

"Kenny King, public defender to the stars!" Kenny shouted across the vacant lot.

"Why are you lurking in parking lots at nighttime and taking pictures of people?" I asked.

"I'm putting together a timeline. Ol' Kenny here just got himself a police scanner, and I'm hot on the case!"

"Well, you're trespassing on a crime scene so get the heck out of here before I throw you in the clink myself," Hudson threatened.

Kenny scrambled backwards, a look of panic coming over his face. "Hey, we're all friends here." He looked at me. "Wanda, right? Wanda and I go way back!"

"My name is Zora. Zora Wick, and I 'Wanda' you to get the out of here."

"Hey, that was funny!" Kenny said, desperately trying to make a bridge of familiarity.

"Hurry," Hudson growled. "Before I get angry."

"I'll uh, just get back to the street and take pictures from a distance!" Kenny said, rushing out of the parking lot.

"That guy is unbelievable," I muttered to Hudson. "He was the public defender they assigned to me back on the Mobson case."

"Good thing that didn't go to trial, you would have been behind bars for life with that incompetent rat representing you. Come on, let's get down to the station."

We hopped back in the van and drove ten minutes east to the police station. Linda escorted us to the secretary, a lady named Mandy, and we sat down to talk to her.

"How are you doing?" Hudson asked the teary-eyed woman as Linda closed the door to the interview room behind us.

"I'm just struggling to get my head around it all," Mandy said. "I can't believe she's dead, she's really dead. Helen? Everyone loved her."

"Do you think you can talk us through the evening's events?" I asked.

"Sure," Mandy stammered, blotting her tears with a tissue and taking a deep breath to steady her nerves. "It was a pretty typical night, just me and Helen in the building after closing. She usually stayed late on Thursdays to catch up on paperwork. I often stayed behind in case she needed help with anything."

"Do you have a copy of her diary for the day?" Hudson asked. "Who did she see?"

"Her usual clients, I can make a list if you like. Her fiancé stopped by as well actually, around lunch time." Mandy paused as though considering something.

"What is it?" I asked.

"I don't want to get anyone in trouble, but—when he came around, I heard them arguing in the office. I think it was something to do with money."

"You say this was around lunchtime?" Hudson queried. She nodded.

"Anything else unusual happen in the day?" I said.

"No, that was about it," Mandy replied.

"So, let's skip to the end of the day. It's just you and Helen in the building. Talk us through it," I prompted.

"At about six I went up to Helen's office and asked if she needed a hand with anything. She said no, but we chatted for about ten minutes. Just casual talk really. After that I went back down to the reception and headed to the bathroom. I was washing my hands when I heard this terrible, blood-curdling scream. I ran up to Helen's office and then—then I found her dead on the floor. I think I screamed when I saw her."

"Then what happened? Did you hear or see anything?"

"I heard a car pull away quickly. I ran to the window, but I wasn't fast enough to see the vehicle. Then I pulled out my phone and called the police." Mandy closed her eyes and took a long and shuddering breath, clearly struggling to relive the ordeal.

"You say everyone loved Helen," Hudson recapped, "but obviously someone had a problem with her. Any idea who?"

Mandy blotted her eyes again, dabbing back the tears. After a moment of reflection her expression changed. "There was something actually—a note left on Helen's car window about a month ago. It was a threat, something about a grave."

"A threat?" I asked.

She nodded. "I think Helen filed a police report, she was unsettled by it."

Hudson pushed his chair back and stood up. "I'll go and check in with Linda, see what she has on file."

"What kind of clients does Helen have?" I asked Mandy.

"A whole variety to be honest. Most of them are self-referrals, but some are court-ordered too."

"Court ordered?"

"Yes, people that require some sort of psychological evaluation for one reason or another. Helen was qualified in that sort of thing," Mandy explained.

"Were any of her clients' tradespeople? Motorbike owners?" I asked.

Mandy shook her head as if she had no idea. "I don't know, to be honest. There are people from all walks of life, I don't get a chance to talk to many of them past a basic greeting."

Hudson came back into the interview room, holding a manilla folder. "Got it," he said and sat down at the table. "Filed one month ago, almost to the day." He pulled out the report, along which there was a photograph of the note left on Helen's car. The note, which was handwritten in thick black marker, had the following words written in all caps:

SEE YOU IN THE CEMETARY

"Looks like spelling isn't one of our mysterious note writer's strong suits," I observed, turning my attention back to Mandy. "Any idea who might have left the note?"

"We didn't have any concrete ideas, but it came a few days after one of her clients exploded in a session. He was a court-ordered client, and I know he'd been referred to have access to his children, I think it was a problem with anger management. Helen had several sessions with him, and the information she passed back to the court wasn't favorable."

Hudson and I looked at one another. "Would you be able to pick this guy's name out of her diary?" he asked.

"No need, I remember it, it was Oscar Mendel."

Hudson wrote the name down and we exchanged another glance. Although neither of us had said anything out loud, I already knew this was our first suspect.

"You mentioned you overheard Helen fighting with her fiancé about money," I recalled. "Was this an everyday run-of-the-mill fight, or did it sound more serious?"

Mandy tilted her head from side-to-side while considering the question. "It's difficult to say because I only heard parts of the argument, but it did sound pretty heated."

"Did they argue often?" Hudson asked.

"I can't really say, he didn't come to the office all that much. I've only met him a few times, but I've never heard them arguing before."

Still, arguing with his fiancée a few hours before her death meant that this guy was a suspect too. "What's his name?" I asked Mandy.

"It's Howard. Howard Price," she said. Hudson too jotted this down.

"Was there anything else you noticed? Anything unusual when you found the body?"

Mandy thought about it for a long moment and then something did come to her. "Actually, now that you mention it, yes. Her necklace was missing. A large platinum pendant! Do you think someone stole it?"

"It's a possibility," Hudson said, making note of the missing necklace.

"You're going to find out who did this, right?" she gulped, tears brimming once more in her eyes. "Helen was an angel; I can't understand why anyone would want her—want her dead!"

At this point Mandy started sobbing again. I sat there awkwardly, not really knowing what to do. Emotionally reassuring people wasn't exactly a skill of mine.

"We're going to find them," Hudson said confidently. "And we're going to make sure they pay for what they've done to—"

Just then Linda came into the interview room, a phone in her hand. "Wick! It's Burt on the line for you. Says it's important!"

"Excuse me," I said to Mandy. I left the room and took the phone from Linda.

"Burt?"

"Wick you can rest easy on this one. We already have the guy," Burt said assuredly.

"You did?" I asked with surprise. "How?"

"That call I responded to about a vagrant in the park? The one with the stolen jewelry?"

"Yeah?" I asked in a prompting tone.

"It's a match. It was a pendant in his hand, with an engraving on the back. *'To Helen, you are my sun and stars – Howard.'* The pendant belonged to the therapist! The guy in the park killed her and went back to his bench to catch forty winks."

"That's... that's crazy," I said, still dumbfounded the case was open and closed this fast. "Who was the guy on the bench?"

"You've probably seen him around, he's always in the park playing his horn for tips. Anyway, we woke him up and he starts freaking out, claiming he knows nothing about the pendant," Burt said casually.

"Hold on a second, what's his name?"

"What do they call him, Wayne? Trombone Joe?" Burt asked. I heard Wayne correct him in the background.

"Saxophone Joe, dad," Wayne said.

"Saxophone Joe?" I gasped.

"That's the one!" Burt said. "Anyway, we're bringing him to the station now. You know him, Wick?"

I just stood there with my mouth hanging open. Saxophone Joe, one of my favorite regulars at the bakery, and one of the nicest people I'd ever met, had just been arrested for murder. Could it actually have been him?

"There's no way Burt..." I said down the phone. "It wasn't him!"

Burt just laughed. "Wick you're out of your mind. We'll be there in a jiffy. You can ask the man yourself!" Burt ended the call and I stared at the blank wall ahead of me.

Something had gone terribly wrong.

CHAPTER 8

"Zora? Miss Zora Wick?" Saxophone Joe said in confusion as he saw me walk into the interview room with Hudson.

"Hey Joe," I sighed, sitting down at the table. "How are things?"

"Not so good, Miss Wick," he said, looking like he'd rather be anywhere else. "I'm surprised to see you here, though to be honest I'm glad—there's no one else I'd rather have looking into this!"

"Joe, you're caught up in a whole heap of trouble. Sheriff Burt thinks you're the one that killed this poor lady," I recapped. "They found you sleeping in the park with her pendant in your hand."

"That necklace? I have no idea how that thing got there, honestly! I've been in the park all night. You can ask any of the other guys!" Joe said desperately.

"Relax, it's okay," Hudson said in reassurance. "We're just trying to get a timeline down. Zora believes quite firmly you aren't our guy."

Joe looked at me with hope. "Really Miss Wick? You believe me?"

"Joe, I don't think you could hurt a fly, but we have to take this seriously. How *did* that pendant get in your hand?"

He shook his head as he tried to think up an answer. "I don't know. I think someone must have placed it there. I'm not a thief, Miss Wick, I've never been in trouble my whole life."

"It's true," Hudson reiterated, though I didn't need him to. Joe had a good energy, I believed him. "He doesn't have a single police file."

"I didn't even know this lady," Joe added. "Never even met her!"

"Actually, you did," I contradicted, as much as I disliked it.

"I did?" Joe asked, his brow knitting in confusion.

I nodded. "Yes, though only very briefly. You held the door open for her when you left my bakery."

Joe's mouth opened very slowly as realization came upon him. "That was her?!"

"It was. You even said she was a 'very beautiful lady'," I recalled.

Joe looked up at the ceiling and rolled his lips together. "I swear to you Miss Wick, I don't know how that necklace got in my hand, but I didn't hurt that lady. Heck, I never even saw her again after leaving your bakery."

I sighed a very long sigh. I knew in my heart of hearts that Joe wasn't our man, but I also knew that from Sheriff Burt's perspective this case was as good as done.

"Do you have a driver's license?" Hudson asked Joe.

"No, when I came up here from New Orleans, I took the Greyhound. Never had the money or need to drive."

"Not even a motorbike?" he asked.

Joe laughed. "Now where am I going to store a motorbike? I live in the park most of the time!"

"You could have boosted one," Hudson suggested, "...but I think I agree with you on this one Zora." Hudson was clutching at straws, and he knew it.

"Whatever I need to do to get out of here, I'll do it," Joe said. "I'm willing to help however I can."

"Zora, any ideas?" Hudson said, looking at me.

I tried to think how I could get Joe out of here tonight, but nothing came to mind. "I can only think of taking a hand-writing sample." It would rule Joe out as the author of the mysterious threat left on Helen's car at least.

Joe looked confused. "Handwriting? I don't understand how that will help."

"That's because you're innocent. Still, we'll take one, nonetheless. We need everything we can get at the moment to make your case look good." I pulled out my phone and searched the news for an article, making sure that it contained the word 'cemetery'. I found a story about local church restorations, copied three paragraphs into my notes app and emailed a copy to Hudson.

"Read that to Joe and get him to write it down. Don't let him see the text," I said as I got up out of my chair. "Joe I'll do everything I can to clear your name, though I don't think there's much chance of you sleeping outside tonight."

He nodded as though he understood. "That's okay. I know you'll save me, Miss Wick."

"Let me know when you're done," I said to Hudson. "I'll wait outside, I need to call Zelda and tell her about Helen." A call I wasn't looking forward to.

"Will do," Hudson affirmed.

I went into the corridor outside, pulled out my phone and called Zelda. I thought there was a chance it might be too late, but she answered.

"I just had the weirdest dream," she said.

"Sorry, did I wake you?"

"No, I fell asleep on the couch but woke up right before you called. I saw my therapist. She said she had to go, but she was proud of all the progress I've made. It's weird, it almost felt like she was moving on!"

"Uh…" I said, drawing the sound out over a long and uncomfortable syllable. Zelda seemed to guess what was coming next.

"No!"

"Why don't I come over and talk to you in person?" I suggested.

"She died?!"

"I wanted to tell you face to face. Can I come over?"

"What happened?" Zelda pressed.

I let out a breath before answering. "She was murdered. We don't know who yet. I'm looking into it. I'll come over and we can talk."

"No, no it's okay," Zelda said. She was trying to sound composed, but I could hear her emotion over the phone. "Thanks for telling me, Z. I think I need some time to process this."

"Okay, well… call me if you need me. I'll see you tomorrow?"

"Yeah, yeah, sure," she said in a dazed manner. "Good night."

I went to say goodnight back, but Zelda had already hung up. Just as I finished the call Hudson came out of the interview room, holding the hand-written note.

"Got the writing sample, want to see it?" he asked, holding up the note. I took one quick glance at it and shook my head.

"No, it's fine, Joe didn't leave the written threat."

"What?!" Hudson said in confusion. "You barely looked at the thing, how can you know?"

I took the note off Hudson and pointed to the word cemetery. "He spelled cemetery correctly. Whoever left the threatening note on Helen's car spelled it 'cemetary'. The rest of the sample doesn't really matter."

"Alright, I'll admit I'm impressed. So, what do we do now?" Hudson asked.

A flabbergasted sigh escaped me—something I seemed to do a lot lately—and I pushed my fingers through my hair. "I don't know, go home and get some sleep? We can pick this up again tomorrow. We've got the name of her fiancé and the client with the anger issues."

"We'll get to the bottom of this," Hudson said with assurance. "We'll clear your friend's name."

"Yeah," I said, though the words were laced with an edge of doubt. In my heart I knew that Joe wasn't the one to kill this woman, but right now I could only state one thing with certainty:

Things didn't look good for Saxophone Joe.

***

THE NEXT DAY I took the morning off from the bakery and went over to Celeste and Zelda's café to see how things were going. When I arrived there, I was surprised to find Zelda working inside along with Celeste. I headed on in and they both nodded at me in acknowledgement. The café was fairly busy for this time of morning, a mix of people having late breakfasts or early lunches—I couldn't tell which.

"What are you doing here?" Zelda asked in surprise.

"Good to see you too," I smirked.

"I just thought you'd be at the bakery is all."

"The bakery is in the hands of Daphne and Rosie today. I'm heading to the station to meet Hudson; we're chasing down suspects." I waited at the side while Zelda saw to a customer. Celeste was acting as the chef this morning, cooking up the orders while Zelda wrote them down and took them to the tables.

"How's she been?" I whispered to Celeste. "The victim was her therapist."

"I heard, and she's being unusually normal," Celeste whispered back. "I think she's in shock."

"I'm not in shock," Zelda said, turning around on her heels as she slapped another order down for Celeste. "I'm just taking each day as it comes. Helen told me to do that actually. I'm not going to call in sick and mope around in bed—that would undo all the progress I've made. I'm soldiering on because of her, and yes, I'm obviously upset. Zora, I really hope you catch whoever did it."

"Don't the police already have a man?" Celeste asked.

"What?!" Zelda said with alarm.

"Where did you hear that?" I said to Celeste. She suddenly looked like she had said something wrong.

"What? It's just a rumor I heard."

"Where, where did you hear this rumor?" I grilled.

"It may have been Constance..." Celeste admitted.

"Well that's the last thing I need, Constance floating around town spreading gossip."

"Is it true then?" Zelda asked me. "Do they have a man?"

"They do, but it's not him. It just... looks significantly like it might be him. But it's not."

Now Zelda looked confused. "What? What does that mean? How can you be so sure it's not him?"

"It's Saxophone Joe," I said with a sigh. "They caught him sleeping in the park with Helen's necklace in his hand."

Zelda's mouth dropped. "Her necklace? Her necklace! That dirty, rotten, scoundrel! He killed her over a necklace?!" At this point Zelda was shouting, and everyone in the café had fallen quiet and was looking at her. "Uh… rehearsing lines for a play!" she laughed nervously, waiting until the patrons turned their attention back to their meals and conversations.

"Joe didn't do it," I stressed. "You've met him. He's a nice guy!"

"I don't know him like you do. I've only met him twice, and he *is* homeless. They kill for money all the time!" Zelda yapped.

"They're still humans, Zelda," Celeste pointed out, throwing in a disapproving look for good measure. I found myself mirroring that look. I knew that Zelda didn't usually harbor anything against the homeless—heck, she even volunteered down at the shelter regularly enough—but she was still hurting about the loss of her friend, and she was determined to get justice.

"You're too close to this to see things logically," I said. "Saxophone Joe has no criminal history *at all*, and I *know* that he's innocent. I can feel it. Call it intuition."

Zelda pouted, but I knew that she valued my judgement. "Well, who did it then?"

"Hudson and I have two leads at the moment. I promise we'll figure this all out; we just have to—" I paused as a familiar figure came into the café. Tall, pale, gaunt, with greasy black hair and hollow eyes. He creeped me out as much as he did when I first met him yesterday. "Oh brother, not this guy again," I muttered under his breath.

"Who is it?" Zelda whispered. "Is he one of the suspects?!"

"He's a hot suspect," Celeste muttered vacantly. I, wondering if we were staring at the same greasy freak, gave her a bewildered look just as Zelda shot an elbow into her ribs. "Ow!" Celeste hissed. "What was that for?!"

"Don't call Helen's killer hot!" Zelda scowled.

"He's not Helen's killer," I said, although he definitely had the aura of someone untrustworthy. "His name is Niles, he's Blake's temporary replacement while Blake is out in the woods sorting out pack politics. He's supposed to be my guardian, but to be honest he just creeps me out."

Niles came right up to the counter and nodded at me with indifference. "Hi," he said in his toneless manner, his hands in his pockets.

"Hey again," I said awkwardly. "Can I help you with something?"

"Aren't you going to introduce me to your friends?"

I looked over at Zelda and Celeste. Zelda was giving Niles a wary look, just as I had yesterday, but Celeste was staring in a rather unusual way. I noticed Niles was looking at her too. "Don't you already know their names?" I asked. "Being my guardian stalker and all?"

"I do, but it wouldn't kill you to have some manners," Niles pointed out. "This is your younger half-sister, Zelda. And this, this charming young woman—" he said, looking at Celeste.

Celeste blushed and laughed nervously. "Charming! He said charming!"

"You're Celeste Wick," Niles said, and for a moment I could swear I even saw a smile on his expressionless creep face. "I've read through all of Blake's files on Zora and her friends, and yours was definitely the most interesting."

"Oh, I doubt that!" Celeste laughed, immediately turning the color of a beetroot.

"Wait a second, Blake has files on us?" I asked.

"I want to see mine. What does it say in mine?" Zelda asked. "It'd better be good."

Niles ignored both of our questions. "I'm supposed to sort of stay in the background and stay out of sight, but I had to come and say hello," Niles said to Celeste. "So... hello."

Celeste responded with another round of nervous laughter and blurted back a, "Hello!"

"I'd like to go out on a date with you sometime," Niles said, pulling something out of his jacket.

"Look out, he's got a—!" I began, stopping myself as Niles

produced a folded-up leaflet. He placed it down on the counter and wrote his number across it.

"Wait, is that a leaflet for a funeral home?" Zelda asked.

"That's a pretty weird thing to write your number on," I pointed out.

Celeste, however, took no notice. She stared at Niles, her mouth still hanging wide open, and took the leaflet from him.

"Call me," he said to her.

"I—I'd like that very much," she stammered back in response.

After another few seconds of uncomfortable staring Niles finally tore his eyes away from Celeste and he looked at me, an expression of misery returning to his gaunt face. "I've got an update for you by the way, there's a weird guy following you."

"Yes, I know, his name is Niles."

Niles just glared at me. "Very funny. Actually, his name is King, Kenny King. Some slimeball lawyer. He seems pretty harmless, but he *is* shadowing you. I thought you'd want a heads up. Anyway, I better get back to work." Niles looked at Celeste again and smiled. "See you soon."

"Bye Niles!" she called as he left the shop. When he was gone Zelda and I just stared at our cousin like she was mad. "What?!" Celeste said, picking up the vibe.

"Really, Celeste? That guy? "He looks like a possessed coat rack!" Zelda said, throwing her hands in the air. I almost choked while taking a sip of my tea.

"She's got a point, Celeste, I get super creepy vibes from him." I wiped my hand over my mouth and put my cup down.

"I should have known the two of you would fail to be happy for me. A hot guy literally walks in off the street and asks to take me out, and all you can do is talk about how much you hate him! Typical!" Celeste turned around and got back to work.

"We're playing fast and loose with the word 'hot' here," I mumbled. "Niles is more in the 'is that guy going to kill me' camp."

"Or 'least popular kid in vampire school' camp," Zelda offered. Once again, I choked on my drink.

"Stop being mean," Celeste said. "Everyone has a type. Zora likes boneheaded alphas, and Zelda, you can't even tell your own ex that you're still in love with him, so I think the pair of you are hardly qualified to start dissecting my love life. I happen to think Niles is a very lovely looking boy, and I can't wait to go on a date with him."

Zelda put on a gruff voice then, trying to make herself sound like one of those commentators from a true crime documentary. "And then, three days later, they found her body face-down in the local creek."

My third consecutive sip of tea sprayed across the counter.

"Alright Zora, time to go," Celeste said. "And Zelda, get back to work!"

"Can I have a grilled cheese before I hit the road?" I asked.

"No, get out!" Celeste barked.

CHAPTER 9

"So, who is this guy?" I asked Hudson as we drove to meet our first suspect.

"Oscar Mendel," Hudson said, reading from the open file in his lap. "Self-proclaimed 'Carpet King' of Compass Cove."

"Is that a heavily disputed title? I mean, I can't imagine many people are gunning for that throne."

Hudson smirked. "Be that the case or not, Mendel does seem to be at the top of the carpet business here in town. His retail warehouse has been recognized as 'Carpet Retailer of the Year' every year for the last five years by 'Good Carpet Buyer Guide' and he's been in the newspaper plenty of times for charity work."

I let out a long whistle, pretending I was overly impressed with the accolades. "You know it's legitimate if Good Carpet Buyer Guide says so, they're the only people I trust when it comes to picking a carpet retailer."

"Personally, I wait to see what the Annual Carpet Awards has to say first before I do any purchasing," Hudson joked back.

"Joking aside, it seems like this guy is something of a pillar in the local community, no?" I asked as I turned off the main street and followed the GPS on my phone.

"It certainly looks that way. Or he's doing his hardest to come across like that at the least."

"So why is he a suspect?" I asked.

Hudson flicked through a few more pages before pulling out a particular piece of paperwork from the file. "This baby, a 73-B-11."

"Ah the old 73-B-11," I said as though as I was recalling the name of a treasured old memory. "If I had a nickel for every time that bad boy came up."

"You have no idea what this form is for, do you?" Hudson grinned.

"Hudson my darling, I haven't the foggiest idea," I said frankly. "What is it?"

"It's a form to signify loss of custody, co-signed by none other than our victim, Helen Bowen, only a few weeks before she died. Oscar Mendel reportedly has troubles with his temper. His wife is in the process of separating from him and filed a court order against Mendel to stop him from seeing his kids. The judge delayed the order pending a psychiatric evaluation, which Bowen signed off after a few sessions with Mendel."

"So, Mendel had a few court-appointed sessions with Helen to prove he wasn't a hot head, failed to do so, she reported her findings, and the court took away the access to his kids," I surmised.

"Bingo," Hudson said. "I can imagine this Oscar Mendel would be pretty angry about that and looking for someone to blame."

"What date was this document signed?" I asked.

"Uh… the 15th," Hudson read.

"One day before the mysterious note was found on Helen's car," I said, glancing over at Hudson. I pulled the van into the parking lot in front of 'Carpet Castle', a large medieval themed warehouse with a fake castle front and an inflatable dragon perched on the roof.

"Let's see what this Oscar Mendel has to say for himself then," Hudson said as we got out of the van.

We headed inside to find a sleepy carpet warehouse with dreary muzak floating over the air. A girl wearing a medieval tabard greeted us half-heartedly from the reception counter. "Welcome to Carpet

Castle, were we slay the competition with our low, low prices. How may I help you today?" she said robotically.

"My name is Zora Wick, and this is Hudson Beck. We're looking for Oscar Mendel, is he around?"

"Are you cops?" the girl gulped.

"No, independent investigators," I answered. It sounded better than 'nosy busybody' at the least. "It's related to the murder of Helen Bowen."

The sleepy-looking receptionist suddenly went wide-eyed upon hearing the word 'murder.'"

"Uh, I'll just find out where he is!" she sputtered, picking up the phone and dialing a number. Hudson and I decided to wander around while the girl located her boss.

"I could do with getting new carpeting for the apartment," I said to Hudson as we flicked through a sample book of high-thread carpets. "The floors in Constance's old apartment are threadbare."

"Hypothetical situation," Hudson proposed. "We find out this guy is the murderer and you're still looking for new carpets. Do you still use his business?"

"I guess that depends."

"On?"

"If the low, low prices really do slay the competition."

Hudson laughed. "I'd probably shop elsewhere, if it was me."

"I think I would too, for what it's worth. This *is* a pretty good deal though. That price for high-thread Egyptian weave? What a bargain."

"And I'll cut you an even better deal if you sign the dotted line today," someone behind us said. Turning around I saw a large, tanned man in boots, beat up jeans, and an old white t-shirt. He had a toolbox in one hand and a phone in the other. "Oscar Mendel, just got back from a fitting. Rebecca mentioned two detectives were here to see me."

"Not detectives," Hudson corrected. "Independent investigators. We're working with the police as an external party."

"Is that so? Well, what is it you wanted to talk about?" he asked.

"We'd like to talk to you about Helen Bowen," I said. "She was murdered at her office last night." As I delivered the news, I studied Mendel's face very carefully, waiting to see if he betrayed any hidden emotions.

He paled a little and his mouth dropped open. "My goodness, that's terrible, I had no idea. Of course, we can talk. If you don't mind me asking, why do you want to talk with me?"

"You were one of her most recent clients," Hudson said. "We're talking to everyone that interacted with Helen recently. We need to collect as much information as possible."

"I see, I see," he nodded, smoothing one hand over his stubbled chin. "Well, let's talk in my office then. Would you like coffee?"

"Sure," I said, and we followed Oscar Mendel across the floor to his office at the back of the shop.

"Aren't you a bit above it now?" Hudson asked Mendel as we walked into his office.

Mendel looked back at Hudson quizzically. "I'm sorry?"

"You said you were out on a fitting," Hudson remarked and nodded at Mendel's toolbox. "I didn't figure the CEO of a successful carpet business would still be doing the fitting jobs."

"Ah," Mendel said with a laugh. We stepped inside his office and sat down at his desk. "I still go out on fitting jobs every now and then, it's quite satisfying work, and sitting here doing paperwork all day can get boring."

A moment later the girl from the reception counter came in with three coffees. We thanked her and she left.

"So, what happened to the therapist? I didn't have that many sessions with her, but she was a nice woman. I'm honestly very surprised someone would want to hurt her," Oscar said and sipped his coffee.

"She was attacked last night in her office, we have no witnesses, but the attacker did leave the murder weapon at the scene, some sort of chisel. Perhaps you recognize it?" I pulled out the file we had and slid a photo of the weapon across the table.

Oscar studied it for a moment and shook his head. "No, though it sure looks like a chisel alright," he said, handing the photo back.

"Where were you last night, between the hours of six and ten?" I said to the Carpet King.

"That's easy, I was at home, working on my car. Got an old Pontiac Firebird that I'm restoring from scratch. She takes up most of my evenings now," Mendel answered.

"Can anyone verify that?" I asked.

Oscar took a sip of his coffee. "I'm pretty sure my neighbors could. My garage door was open all night and I had the Pontiac up on stands." He looked at Hudson as though he'd understand. "Setting up the transmission. Heck of a puzzle."

Hudson laughed in familiarity. "I bet. More of a bike guy myself to be honest. You ride?"

Mendel gave a quick and sharp turn of his head. "Nah, not really. Used to take a dirt bike out on the trails when I was younger, but not much these days."

"So, what was the reason for your therapy sessions with Helen Bowen?" Hudson asked. We, of course, already knew the answer, but asking these sorts of questions was instrumental when talking with a suspect. Was he the type that told the truth? Was he comfortable talking with law-enforcement types? Would he outright lie? Every answer told us something beyond its surface.

Mendel narrowed his eyes at the question and sat back in his seat. He was a large set guy with spiky black hair and a pudgy face. Although he was Caucasian, he had a pretty significant tan at the moment. "I'm not the type to go about airing my dirty laundry," Mendel said, "but my therapy sessions were to do with anger management. I guess you could say I've got a short fuse, and Helen was helping me work through that."

"And would you say you made much progress in managing your anger response?" I probed.

Oscar twisted his mouth as he thought the question over. "We cracked it right open," he said. "All I gotta do is breathe, count to ten, and remember the 'I' statements."

"'I' statements? What's that?" Hudson said, taking a sip of his drink and leaning forward slightly.

"Uh, it's a way of reframing anger. Say someone cuts you off in traffic and you get in an argument about it. Instead of saying 'Hey, you drive like a jackass!', you say, 'Hey, *I think* you drive like a jackass!'" Mendel explained with a knowing grin.

"I'm not sure if that's how 'I' statements are supposed to work," I pointed out.

"Eh, probably not," Mendel accepted. "I have to admit I struggled with parts of the therapy."

"But you cracked it right open, right?" Hudson said, pointing out the changing account.

Mendel gave Hudson a quick look, like the question caught him off guard. "Hey, nobody's perfect, right?" he laughed.

"That's a pretty big fish," I said in a bid to change the topic. I picked up a framed photo on the desk and examined it more closely. In it, Oscar Mendel was standing on a white-sand beach, holding up a large finned-fish that was nearly as long as his body. "That you?"

"Sure is." Mendel leaned in and smiled proudly. "Sailfish, 153lbs. Nearly tore my rotator cuff trying to hold that thing up. Me and my brother go down to Guatemala once a year to fish for a week, just got back from this year's trip actually."

"I can tell from the tan," Hudson remarked. "Almost as impressive as the catch."

Oscar laughed. "Eh well, that fish was a few years ago. Didn't get anything quite as good this time."

"Anyway," Hudson said, leading back into the questions. "We heard you and your wife separated recently, and that the separation wasn't pretty. What can you tell us about that?"

A change came over the Carpet King then, a silent storm of fury stirring in his eyes. I was almost sure he was seconds away from jumping over the table and attacking Hudson at the mention of his wife. "Why exactly was it you wanted to talk to me?" he asked suspiciously. "Because I kind of feel like I'm on the stand here, and I don't think that the business with my wife is relevant."

"We don't mean to make you feel like that," I cut in. "We're just trying to figure out what happened to Helen, you understand?"

"Sure..." Oscar Mendel said, though I could tell now that he was starting to put the boundaries up. "Well, I haven't got all morning you understand, so... are we done here?"

"Not quite," Hudson said. "You see we actually know why you had the therapy sessions with Helen, and we know they didn't go very well. They were court-ordered, and you had to get her approval to keep seeing your kids. The thing is, she signed the papers saying you shouldn't see your kids, so you lost access. That's right, isn't it?"

The Carpet King balled his hands into tight fists, his jaw clenched, and I saw his chest start to rise and fall. "What's the point in asking questions if you already know the answers to them?" Mendel said through his teeth.

"We want to make sure we've got our facts straight," I said. "It's just standard routine."

Mendel took his eyes off Hudson and looked at me. I had no doubt a quiet rage was simmering away underneath the surface, only a few wrong turns from breaking out. "Is that so?" he said. "Well, yeah—as it happens that's how things went. I wasn't happy about it, but I doubt you would be either. Do you have children?"

"No," I said. "I've got a couple of annoying pets though."

"Then you don't understand what it's like. Once you have kids, you'll do anything to keep them. You'd even—"

"Kill?" Hudson interrupted.

Oscar Mendel's tanned face started to turn beet red. "Are you calling me a liar?" he said, his voice starting to sound more like a snarl.

"Not at all," Hudson responded calmly. "And I think you might be forgetting your 'I' statements."

"I think you might be forgetting that I'm talking to you out of kindness. You're not cops, I'm not obligated to say a single word."

"We're all friends here," I said, jumping in to try and calm the waters between Oscar Mendel and Hudson. I knew what Hudson was doing, he was trying to get a rise out of the suspect to and see what it would take to make him snap, but we needed more before he walked away. "Let's just take a breath. Is there a chance we could get a handwriting sample from you?"

Mendel's brow wrinkled in confusion; his anger delayed a few moments longer. "Excuse me? What the heck do you want a handwriting sample for?"

"Just for our records, it will help the case."

He stared at me for a moment as he considered the question, and then his cell phone started ringing on the desk. It made me jump, but Mendel calmly picked it up and answered. "Hello? Okay, I'll be right there, thanks." He put the phone down and pushed his chair back. "I'm sorry, but I'll have to cut our talk short, I have work to get back to."

"What about that sample?" Hudson pressed. "It will only take a minute."

"I'm afraid I haven't got a minute, now if you'll excuse me, it's time to leave." Mendel walked around the desk and opened the door to his office, holding it open and gesturing for us to leave.

Hudson and I got up and left without another word. The Carpet King clearly had a problem with his temper, but was he our murderer?

We still had questions to answer.

CHAPTER 10

We were on our way to grab lunch when Hudson's phone started to buzz. "Ah sheesh," he said, looking at the incoming messages.

"Everything okay?" I asked him.

"I'm going to have to put a hold on the detective work, I just got an incoming job from MAGE. According to our sensors it looks like the kraken at the bottom of the lake might be waking up."

I laughed and slapped my hand on the wheel. "Kraken! That's a good one. Gosh, can you imagine?" After a few moments of silence, I looked over at Hudson and saw that he was being completely serious. "Oh my god, you're not joking?"

"I thought I already mentioned the kraken to you?" he asked, tucking his phone into his pocket.

"I'm pretty sure I would remember something about a giant kraken living at the bottom of Compass Cove lake. How big is it exactly?"

"Oh it's…" Hudson drifted off as though recalling something horrific. "It's pretty big. But the positive note is that it's been asleep for several hundred years. MAGE has had sensors on it for a while, and that thing is in a *very* deep sleep, but the readings have just picked up some brain activity."

"I don't think I'm ever going to sleep well again."

"Don't worry, it's probably just having a bad dream. Either way, I'm going to have to dive down and get a look at the sensors to make sure they're not malfunctioning. Could you drop me off at the harbor?"

"Sure," I said, turning off the street and looping around the block to head in the right direction. "Also, I think you don't always have to tell me about your work. I'd sleep better not knowing."

Hudson chuckled. "I thought you wanted me to be more open about this stuff?"

"Yes, I thought that too, and then I found out that you're about to go diving with a colossal squid, I mean, it's not exactly dog walking, is it?" I pointed out. "What happens if it wakes up? You're pretty much a goner, right?"

"Oh, for sure," he said, nodding in a very certain way. "But you can relax, the kraken isn't going to wake up today, and if it *did*, it would take several days until it was fully awake. It's a very deep sleep."

"But if it woke up you would die," I said.

"Absolutely. The entire town would get flattened to be honest. I don't think many would make it out alive."

I pulled up at the harbor and stared at Hudson for a few long seconds. "This is supposed to make me feel better?"

He chuckled. "I'm just saying, you don't have anything to worry about. Trust me. I've handled a few giant krakens in my time. Most of the time they just want to sleep and be left alone."

"Maybe it's just me, but if I knew a colossal creature was sleeping next to a town, I'd move the creature, or do something about it."

Hudson climbed out of the car and came around to the driver-side window to give me a kiss. "Well you let me know when you figure out how to move a kraken, or the alternative. Best thing to do with these things is just let them sleep."

"And when they wake up?"

Hudson's jovial manner faded a little. "Then you try and get them back to sleep as fast as possible. If you can't do that, evacuate everyone in a one-hundred-mile area and hope for the best."

"Sometimes it worries me that you guys are the ones taking care of this stuff."

Hudson chuckled again and shrugged. "Hey, if you know someone better then give me their details!"

"I'll keep my eyes peeled. Just be careful, okay?"

"I'm always careful!" he said as he walked away from the car. "Are we still doing dinner at yours tonight?"

"Sure thing, see you later."

Once Hudson was out of eyesight, I turned the van around and headed back into town. Next on my list was 'Howard Price', Helen's fiancé whom she had argued with only a few hours before her death. I decided to give him a call before swinging by his house, so I didn't catch him on the back foot, but the call just went to voicemail. "Okay, I'll turn up unannounced then…" I mumbled to myself and put his address into the GPS.

Fifteen minutes later I pulled up outside his house, a nice place in an upmarket suburb. I walked up the path, knocked on the front door and waited—there was no response. Was there a chance he'd gone into work today? The day after his fiancée died? I went back to the van and checked the file, according to Wayne's notes 'Howard Price' was a florist and had a flower shop in town.

Huh. Didn't Tamara say there was some sort of unusual pollen found at the crime scene?

I pulled out my phone and called the number for the flower shop. A woman answered the phone. "Hello, Gilded Lilly, this is Kate speaking, how may I help you?"

"Hi Kate, my name is Zora Wick and I'm working with Compass Cove Police. Is Howard around?"

"Oh gosh," the girl responded, sounding like she was on the verge of tears. "It's so awful what happened to Helen. Howard isn't in today, he's taken a personal day, understandably so."

"Of course. Did he mention where he was going? I need to talk to him and he's not at home."

"Gosh, I don't know. Do you have his cell phone number? Maybe try that?"

Already been there. No dice. "Alright, thanks for your time."

I hung up the phone and immediately tried Howard Price again, but there was still no answer. I left a voicemail and then I called the police station.

"Compass Cove police station, Linda Combs speaking. How may I direct your call?"

"Hey Linda, can I speak with Burt? I think a suspect might have disappeared."

"Well that depends, *Zora Wick*," Linda said mysteriously. She was a large woman with a fondness for crossword puzzles and every time I wanted something from her there was usually a catch.

"On what?" I asked. "This is serious! It's for a murder investigation!"

"Eight down... Something unpalatable," Linda said, dropping the clue that she was stuck on.

"Linda, seriously. Just put me through to Burt. This is professional police work!"

Linda snorted in response. "Then I guess I'll just put the phone down, how about that?"

I sighed and held a fist against my forehead. "It's a miracle anything ever gets done in this town, you know that?"

"I'm still waiting," Linda said, sounding like she was growing quickly bored of the conversation.

"It's *inedible*, you ingrate. Something unpalatable. *Inedible!* Come on, it's not hard!"

"Now, now, no need to get snappy about it! Let me see if Burt is in the station—"

"Wait a second, you put me through all that and you don't even know if he's in the building?! This is the last time I—!"

"Hold please!" Linda sang mischievously. Her voice clicked away and hold music came over the line. I stood there for a good minute, wondering what I'd done in a past life to deserve this sort of treatment. The music clicked away as Linda came back. "Zora?"

"Yes, Linda?" I said through my teeth.

"Burt's in his office. I'll just put you through now. Providing you can tell me the answer to this one, it's—"

"Linda!" I said shrilly.

"Relax!" she said, laughing wildly down the phone. "I'm just pushing your buttons, sugar. I'll put you through now." Another click followed and then I heard Burt's voice.

"Wick? What's going on?" he asked. "Don't tell me you've tripped over another damn body."

"No, I'm looking into the Helen Bowen case, I'm trying to track down her fiancé but he's not around. Any idea where he might be?"

"Wick, why in the name of Shakira are you trying to track down her fiancé? I already told you the case is done and closed. We got our man! It was the hobo from the park. He had her jewelry for Pete's sake!"

"His name is Saxophone Joe, and I'm telling you Burt, I don't think he's our man. I know Joe, he's a good guy, he wouldn't do something like this!" I protested.

"Listen Wick," Burt said with a regretful sigh. "I think I know what's happening here."

"You do?" I asked, not understanding where he was going with this.

"Yeah, I guess it's kind of my fault. I've been dangling these checks in front of you, promising you riches in return for your hard work. Look, I know it's exciting to be making a living off your smarts, heck, it's the same reason I got into police work."

An uncomfortable silence stretched between us. "Uh…"

"But you can't just run around town billing hours for a mystery that's already solved. I know, *I know*, the money is enticing. But we ain't a charity farm, Zora, bank notes don't grow on trees—though I guess the paper *does* come from trees—"

"I'm not doing this for the money you nitwit, I'm doing it because I don't think this case is closed. I don't care about the cash. Don't pay me, I'm doing this to clear Saxophone Joe's name!"

Burt was silent for a second. "Alright then, as long as you understand there's no cash for a closed case."

"Lord, give me strength," I muttered under my breath. "Howard Price, Helen's fiancé. Where is he? He's not at home, not at work, and he's not answering his phone."

"If I was betting man, I'd say it sounded like he skipped town," Burt remarked.

"Yeah, I'm getting that vibe myself, which makes him look incredibly guilty, don't you think? Has anyone at the station talked to him yet?"

"Let's see here..." Burt said, and in the background, I heard the rustle of paperwork. "Yeah, looks like Wayne and Zayne visited him briefly at the house to take a statement. He didn't mention anything about going anywhere. We usually tell folks to stay put when an active investigation is underway. Not that this investigation is active anymore," he added.

"Put me through to Wayne or Zayne, I want to hear what went down."

After muttering something about 'wasting time', Burt fumbled his way through the phone controls and a new voice came over the line.

"Ahoy hoy?" Wayne said.

"You went to Howard Price's house last night. How did he seem?"

"Pretty beat up, but you know, his fiancé did just die. He took the news pretty badly."

"Why not take him back to the station for a statement?" I asked.

"The guy was a mess, Zora. I told him we'd do the talk tomorrow. Give him time to get his thoughts together. That was before we caught that other guy down at the park though."

"Has anyone in this police station completed formal police training?" I asked in exasperation.

"In my defense there's a lot of training. Do you know there's like 78 genders now? That's a lot of different ways I can accidentally insult people. We gotta walk on eggshells these days," Wayne complained.

"I think Howard Price has done a runner. Did he give you that vibe at all?"

Wayne took a few long moments to think about it. "You know I could see him doing that. Sure seems like the type. Why run though? We already got the killer. And why are you still working this case? You know daddy ain't gonna cut you a check for a case that's closed!"

"I'm going to hang up now before I scream. Goodbye Wayne."

With that I ended the call and shoved the phone into my pocket. I started walking back to the van when a car pulled up on the drive of Howard's neighbor. A man got out and waved.

"Morning!" he said heartily.

I didn't return the warm greeting, but I did zone in on him for information. "Howard Price. Where is he?" I asked.

The directness took the man back a little. "Uh, fishing, I think?"

"You think?"

"I saw him pack his things up this morning. Looked like he was going camping or something."

"Did he mention where?" I asked.

The man shook his head. "No, why, is he in trouble?"

With that I walked back to the van, shut the door behind me and started the engine.

One of our suspects had vanished into thin air. This definitely wasn't the open and shut case that Burt claimed it to be.

CHAPTER 11

"Still no answer," Hermes said the next morning over the kitchen table. I had Hermes on 'get Howard to answer his phone' duty, which consisted of him tapping the redial button on my phone every couple of minutes with his little kitty paw.

"How many is that?" I asked while making myself a quick breakfast.

"That's 23 attempts this morning."

"I've been thinking," Constance announced as she floated into the room.

"Crikey, here we go," I muttered to myself. I then put on a smile and with my most cheery effort I greeted her. "Good morning, Constance! What have you been thinking about?"

"I don't get enough respect around here," she said flatly.

"Attempt 24, still no answer," Hermes repeated.

"Exhibit A!" Constance said dramatically, thrusting her hands in Hermes direction. "I float in and not even the slightest bit of acknowledgement from my old familiar!"

"Hermes give Constance some slight acknowledgement," I said to him while buttering my toast.

"Huh?" he said, lifting his head to look at the ghost of his old owner. "Oh, you're here," he said with disinterest.

"Exhibit number B!" Constance wailed.

"I don't think you say number if you're using the alphabet," I said, taking my tea and toast over to the table.

"Attempt 25, don't drink and drive," Hermes said.

"What?" I asked in confusion.

"This job is getting pretty boring, so I'm spicing it up a little bit, thought I'd make myself sound like one of those old-fashioned bingo callers."

"I guess I'll just go and kill myself," Constance said. "I'll throw myself off a bridge and end it all."

"You're already dead," I pointed out. "So, this is literally the most transparent cry for attention *ever*."

"Doubly so because she's a ghost," Hermes muttered while trying Howard's phone. "Because she's a ghost? Get it? Ghosts are transparent."

"Yes, that was basically the gist of my joke," I said.

"Attempt 26, rocks and sticks."

"Everything here," Constance said, floating down and gesturing at the apartment and the bakery below. "*Everything* here is here because of *me*. I made this. I made all of this!"

"You made this toast?" I asked, taking a bite out of it.

"You made this cheap Chinese knock off phone?" Hermes asked.

"I bought that when I was broke," I said defensively.

"I made the business that allowed you to buy those things!" Constance snapped.

I put my toast down and rubbed my temples. "Where is this coming from? You're usually a lot more bearable than this. What do you want us to do? Build you a shrine?"

Constance crossed her arms. She had the energy of someone that was incensed but didn't really know what they wanted. "Well, that might be a start," she sputtered. "The Japanese ghosts get a lot of respect from their living relatives. They have shrines. And the Mexican ghosts do too!"

"We're not Mexican or Japanese," I pointed out.

"I'm one sixteenth Cherokee," Hermes said. "Attempt 28, garden gate!"

"No, you're not Mexican or Japanese, you're just inconsiderate!" Constance said, throwing her hands up and making her best attempt at crying, which, truth told, was pretty miserable.

"Did something happen last night?" I asked, trying to figure out where this mood was coming from. Constance didn't need to sleep as a ghost, so she and the other ghosts of Compass Cove were free to do as they wished with the night. From what I understood they spent a lot of time socializing at the graveyard. "Did another ghost say something to you?"

"Well, it's funny you should ask, actually," she said, pulling out a chair for herself and floating down into a sitting position. "It was the auditions for the *Cherry Gals*, last night, and I didn't get in."

At this point Hermes looked up from the phone, seemingly giving up on the redial operation. "The Cherry Gals?" he said with disgust. "Why would you audition to be one of them?"

"Because they hold prestige, Hermes, and they are well respected," Constance said haughtily. "Not something you'd understand."

"I think they're a bunch of stuck up—" he began.

"Hold the phone, what's a *Cherry Gal?*" I asked.

"Oh, they're only the most happening ghost lady acapella group in Compass Cove," Constance explained.

"And you auditioned to be one of them?" I asked.

"That's right," she said with a firm nod. "To be a Cherry Gal isn't just to be in a band. They're elegant, they're respected, and they sit on the tomb at the top of the graveyard, like queens overseeing their—"

"They're a bunch of stuck-up snobs," Hermes cut in. "Those old broads drive me up the wall."

"Hermes! Show some respect!" Constance barked. Hermes just stuck his tongue out in response.

"Constance it's much too early in the day for you to come in here shouting at us. Why do you want to be one of these Cherry Gals anyway? You're an awful singer."

"I've been practicing though. Look!" Constance began a rendition of Billy Joel's Piano Man. I'm not sure what key she was in—all of them by the sounds of it—if anything her singing had definitely gotten worse.

"Oh my god," Hermes said, lifting his paws and putting them over his ears. "I've heard plenty of caterwauling in my life, but that takes the crown!"

I motioned for Constance to stop, and she did. "That's... that's enough," I said, wondering if there was a spell to erase the memory of a sound.

"What do you think? It's better, right?"

"The windows didn't crack this time..." I said, trying to be as supportive as I could. "Be honest though, why do you want to be one of these Cherry Gals? You were never interested in singing before. You're not exactly a music lover. I mean, you've got those Donny Osmond posters, but that's about the extent of your musical intrigue."

"Zora, sweet naïve Zora..." Constance said, rolling her eyes and tutting to herself. "I'm not doing it for a 'love of music', I couldn't care less about the music darling."

"Did you open your audition with that?" Hermes asked dryly.

"I'm doing it because I want that prime graveyard retail estate. Those Cherry Gals sit up there on their tomb, looking down over everyone else, thinking they're god's gift to Compass Cove. Well, let me tell you... I won't take it anymore! I'll start my own music group!"

"Please don't," I said.

"You could call yourselves the Cursed Bagpipes, or the Out of Key Banshees," Hermes offered.

Constance just shook her head and floated up from the table. "Like I said. No respect, no respect at all. Well, I'll show you. I'll show all of you! You and the Cherry Gals. Constance will have the last laugh! My musical group will win the Compass Cove ghost choir competition, and then they'll probably make a film about my struggle to the top. Maybe Will Smith will play me?"

"He's kind of taken a dive in popularity recently..." Hermes pointed out.

"He's also a black male. And you're the ghost of a middle-aged white woman," I said. "I can think of better casting choices."

"Well maybe you just do that," she said snippily. "I'm going to go out and start recruiting for my new choir. The Cherry Gals will rue the day they messed with me!" she wailed as she flew through the ceiling.

"Attempt 29, wine and dine," Hermes said.

I took my phone back off him. "I don't think he's answering, do you?"

Hermes shrugged and yawned. "Eh, I don't know. Now I believe you mentioned something about paying me in head scritches?"

"Later, I've got to get ready for my day. On an unrelated note, is there any way to rid a place of an unwanted ghost?"

Hermes smirked. "Anyone I might know?"

"It's just a bit much sometimes," I said. "Like… isn't there somewhere she can move onto to get peace?"

"There is," he said with a nod, "but I don't think she's ready yet. You have to remember that Constance was murdered, so she's probably still trying to resolve *that*."

"I suppose. I feel like she's getting crazier though."

"The thing about ghosts is that the normal ones don't usually hang around that long. People at peace move on, and people with purpose usually reincarnate and go onto do something in their next life. The ones that hang around as ghosts are usually the really annoying ones, or ones with unfinished business."

"Constance ticks both of those boxes though," I remarked.

"Yes, we might be stuck with her for quite some time."

"Is there anything we can do to help the process?"

He shook his head. "There's one surefire way to make a ghost situation worse, and that's by trying to force them out. Don't get me wrong, if it was some random whacko haunting the apartment, we could tell them to respect your space, but as Constance is family *and* used to live here, she has a strong attachment here."

"Surely I can keep her from coming into my bedroom and the bathroom though?"

"Oh, for sure, just tell her to get out and respect your privacy. Ghosts are obligated to respect the living to a certain extent."

"Huh..." I said, relishing the opportunity to try out that new tool. "I'll keep that in mind. Okay, I better get up and going. I need to get ahead of the day." I slurped down the last of my tea and headed into Constance's old bedroom to get an outfit, approaching the magic wardrobe in the corner. "Bungalow," I said, uttering the passphrase.

The wooden face on the wardrobe opened its eyes but the doors didn't open. "Can I help you with something?" the wardrobe asked.

"Yes, I'd like an outfit please. Not as formal as yesterday. Just casual and cool. Smart casual witch, you know?" I laughed at my awkward description and flicked my hair.

"How are we doing with those moth balls I asked for?" the wardrobe said flatly.

"Uh..."

"And that varnish? Hm? Did we forget about those things?"

"I will... get those things sorted today, I promise."

"Promises are funny things," the wardrobe said. "Little meaningless trinkets made up of sounds, completely worthless until their corresponding act is delivered."

"Alright, I get the message. Flipping heck, you and Constance were perfect for each other."

"What's that supposed to mean?" the wardrobe scowled.

"Nothing. Can you just give me a cool chic outfit? I'll go and get your things now. I promise."

"Fine," the wardrobe huffed. "But you don't get a knockout outfit. I'm not giving my best work until you uphold your end of the bargain."

"Fine, just—" Before I could say anything else the doors snapped open quickly and the clothes catapulted into my face. Flustered, I caught them and stared at the wardrobe disapprovingly. "Let's add another caveat to the bargain, stop throwing stuff in my face."

"No need to be a drama queen about it," the wardrobe murmured.

I quickly put on the outfit that the wardrobe had picked out for me. It was nine tenths of the way to being a really cute witch chic outfit—a silky black blouse, a long black skirt with copper flower detail and a pair of...

"White boots? With this outfit?" I asked the wardrobe as I looked at myself in the mirror. "Black boots would look better."

"They would indeed, and once you get my moth balls and varnish, I will start dressing you properly. For now, you get the incomplete package. 8 out of 10 outfits at best, nothing more until you complete the deal!"

8 out of 10 was a pretty apt way of putting it. Plenty of times I felt like one item of clothing was throwing off the rest of my outfit. I had to give it to wardrobe, she really knew how to light a fire under me.

I huffed my thanks and went back into the apartment. "Really?" Hermes asked as I went for the door. "Those boots with that outfit?"

"Don't you start," I said. "Stay out of trouble and look after the apartment, okay?"

"I'll try and do *one* of those things. Have a good day!"

I headed downstairs and had a quick chat with Daphne and Sabrina, who had taken care of the morning bake and opened the bakery. After catching up I went out to the van and saw that Zelda was ringing me.

"Sup?" I answered.

"I need to go to the mall. Do you want to come?"

"As a matter of fact, I do. What are you getting at the mall?"

"I'm going to get my eyebrows threaded. I figured that if Will notices, that means he's in love with me and things between us are still on," she said.

"He literally asked you out the other day and *you* said no."

"I already told you that I panicked. Now he's going on another date with that other harlot! He thinks I just want to be friends. If he notices my new brows, then he's still into me."

"...Is there lead in your water? I'm asking honestly. Just tell him how you feel."

Zelda scoffed down the line. "And *I'm* the one that sounds crazy. Are you driving? Pick me up from the café, I went there for breakfast."

"I'll be right over. Maybe on the way I can call Will and let him know how you really feel."

"If you do that, I will *never* talk to you again! Just leave it to me, I know what I'm doing."

"Right… it's just that he literally asked you out on a date, and now you're literally ripping your eyebrows out to try and get his attention."

"Well, when you put it like that it *does* sound crazy. Trust me Zora, I know what I'm doing."

"Aging me prematurely? Mission accomplished. Tell Celeste I'll take a bacon and egg sandwich to go." Zelda relayed the order over the line.

"She says you need to apologize to Niles first for being mean to him."

"That creep?! I'll never apologize! Tell *her* she needs to be careful around him. It won't be long until she ends up as a souvenir in his serial killer drawer!"

Zelda too relayed that info. "Celeste says you're banned from the café until further notice."

"You know what, I'll get my own bacon and egg sandwich from somewhere else. I dare say there'll be less grief!"

"Whatever, just hurry up and get over here," Zelda said, "If I get the brows sorted before ten, Will and I might be engaged by Christmas, and then my life will almost be back on track."

"I'm surrounded by lunatics. I'm surrounded by lunatics," I repeated to myself. I swear sometimes it felt like I was the only normal person around here, which admittedly sounded like *I* was the crazy one, but you only had to spend an afternoon with my family to see the truth.

Wick women were cursed with a certain brand of madness. Did I have it too?

CHAPTER 12

Despite having lived in Compass Cove for some time now, I'd not actually been to the mall yet, so I was somewhat excited about our impromptu shopping trip.

"Okay," Zelda said as we walked into the mall's main atrium. "Brenda's Brow Stall is that way," she said, pointing to the left. "Where are you going again?"

I'd briefly searched the internet before coming here and found a special furniture replacement specialist located in the mall. "Chang's Restorations," I said, recalling the name of the business.

"Never heard of it, but okay. Meet back here in thirty minutes? We can get a pretzel and a shake before we leave."

"Sounds perfect, I'll see you then."

We went our separate ways, Zelda voluntarily heading towards her brow torture, and myself walking to the nearest map to figure out where my furniture place was. After a quick inspection of the map, it seemed my destination was on the third floor, towards the back of the mall. With a skip in my step and a jaunty whistle I set off across the mall.

About ten minutes and several escalators later I found the old furniture shop. While the rest of the mall was bright and airy, the third floor was dim, dusty and unnervingly quiet. Chang's Restorations was one of the only shops open up here, the rest of them had metal shutters down over their fronts, a signal that perhaps enough shoppers didn't come up here to make it profitable.

I stepped into the cluttered store, a heap of dark walnut antiques, emerald dragon statues and ethnic trinkets. An incense stick was burning away on a countertop at the back of store, a station which was currently unmanned. I rang the bell and almost straight away an old Asian man with a long silver moustache stepped through a bead-curtain door. He was wearing an outfit made of red silk, with yellow patterns embroidered across the fabric.

His eyes were strangely dark, and as he came into my presence the hairs stood up on the back of my neck. "Yes?" he said, clasping his hands behind his back.

"Uh…" I began slowly, wondering if I had made some sort of mistake coming in here. I looked back to the shop's entrance, which felt very far away now that I was in the heart of the establishment. My fingertips began to crackle with the presence of magical energy, and I realized that this was no ordinary shop. "I have this wardrobe…"

"Oh?" the old man said, one of his bristly white brows lifting slightly on his forehead. "And I'm guessing it's not an *ordinary* wardrobe," he said, in a manner that suggested we were both speaking about magic.

"That's right. In fact, she's grown to be quite stubborn. She's demanding mothballs and a new lacquer of varnish."

A grin spread across the old man's face, and he laughed. "Sounds about right. Magical wardrobes can be very handy, but they can also have quite the temper. I take it you require the assistance of a restoration man like myself?"

Again, I knew he was referring to the fact that he was magical. "Yes, but it's just—" I began, cutting myself off before I aired my trepidations. The fact of the matter is that I was getting a very unnerving vibe from this man, and his eyes were so unnaturally dark, I'd never seen anything like it before. I knew that followers of the Sisters of the Shade were lurking in Compass Cove, could it be this old man was one of them?

"It's just that you feel uneasy around me," the old man noted.

I swallowed, wishing I had something to wet my dry throat. "I'm sorry, I don't mean any offense by it. I think I'll go somewhere else."

I'd only just turned to leave again when he spoke up. "You've never been around a divination magician, have you?" he asked.

I stopped and looked back. "I beg your pardon?"

"That's what you're feeling," he explained. "That sickness, that unease, that bile in the back of your throat. Most witches and wizards don't feel at ease around divination witches, and those that are more perceptive, witches like yourself, the effect is even stronger—to a point where it feels unbearable."

I had stepped back a few paces now. If what he was saying was true then I felt a little guilty, but I couldn't help feeling this way. "Like I said, I meant no offense by it. I'll find someone else."

"There is no one else," he said frankly.

Again, I did a doubletake. "I beg your pardon?"

"I am the man that made your magical wardrobe. I made all of them in fact. There are just under one hundred in existence, and I'm the only one with the ability to craft them. Tell me, who do you have?"

"Who do I have?" I repeated, not understanding the question.

"Yes. What is the name of your wardrobe?"

"I don't know its name," I stammered. "It sounds like a posh old English lady, and she has a lot of attitude."

"Ah, that sounds a lot like Eustice," he recalled fondly. "Yes, she was one of my first. A brilliant specimen."

"She has a name?" I asked in bewilderment.

"They all do. Eustice, I believe I sold to a witch that runs a bakery in town. The wardrobe is now in your care?"

"Yes, she died, and she's sort of passed it down to me."

"I see. Well, Eustice is definitely overdue a visit. I can come and see her tomorrow?"

"Uh…" I began again, trying to think of a way to cancel this appointment. Like I said, I didn't want to offend the guy, but I really didn't like the vibe I was getting off him.

"You don't trust me," he said perceptively.

"Don't take it personally. I have the wrong sort after me though, and I have to be very careful about who I let into my home."

"Allow me then to give you a reading," he said.

"A reading?" I asked.

He nodded. "Yes. Most find it helps somewhat with the unnerving feeling. Once the reading is done most find the company of a divination user much more tolerable. You can stay there if you like, you don't have to come any closer. I just need to look into your eyes."

"And if I disagree?" I asked, getting ready to pull out my wand and blast this old guy to kingdom come if I needed to.

He smiled in reassurance. "Trust me, I cannot and would not bring any harm to you, and I would not perform a reading without your permission." The old man then pulled out his wand, a broad flat stick with black symbols carved along the face. Out of instinct I pulled mine out too and his reaction was to laugh.

"Relax, miss! I am giving you my wand to prove you can trust me. See?" He put the wand down on the counter and nodded for me to take it. I did and took a couple of steps back again. "You would have left already if you thought me a threat," he said.

"Constance bought a wardrobe off you, and she can sniff out dark magic better than anyone, so I figure you're probably on the level. Now… what's this reading about?"

"I have your permission?" he asked.

"Yes… but don't make me regret this," I said. "I won't hesitate to cast some unexpected and overpowered magic your way."

"I'm sure you won't!" he laughed. With that the old man put his hands palm side up on the table and then he looked into my eyes. He started muttering some sort of incantation in Chinese. I noticed the wafting smoke from the incense burner was now moving in a strange geometric pattern, and as I looked back to the old man it happened.

In a flash his black eyes changed to white, his hands slammed down on the counter and his body filled with tension. The old man opened his mouth, and a choral voice came out, different from his normal voice.

"Open the eyes, tell me what you see, in your future I see trouble, your traitors number three."

It ended as quickly as it began, the old man's eyes snapping back to black and the tension leaving his body. It was hard to explain, but as his reading ended it felt as though the air in the shop had grown lighter. The strange and nauseous revulsion lifted, and I felt a little more comfortable around the strange old man.

"Well?" he said with a cordial laugh. "I bet you don't feel so sick now, eh?"

"Why does it happen?" I asked, wondering why divination magic would feel so unpleasant until a reading was performed.

"We don't truly know. It might have something to do with the energy us divination magicians carry. The future is uncertain, and we project an energy of overwhelming uncertainty until a person receives their reading."

"I suppose that makes sense, in a rather strange way," I admitted. Whatever the reason was, I felt almost normal again now.

"So, what did I say?" he asked. "Was it good or bad?"

"You don't remember?" I asked with a note of surprise.

"No, that is another curse of the divination magician. We are completely blind to our prophecies. The only ones who may know the future are those not destined to see it."

That alone felt like a riddle in itself. "You uh, you said I had three traitors." I handed his wand back and he took it.

"And from the look on your face I assume that reading makes sense to you?" he asked.

"Unfortunately, yes." I already suspected one person in this town was working with the dark witches to let them slip the town's protective magical boundaries. Could the old man's reading be correct? Could there really be three people working against me?

"Well, I apologize," he said with a note of regret. "Next time I hope I can give you a more positive reading. Now, how about tomorrow morning?"

"Excuse me?" I asked, looking up from the countertop.

"The wardrobe? You wanted it servicing?"

"Oh, I…" I'd completely forgot why I came in here to be honest. "Tomorrow morning is fine. Let me give you my address." I passed the details onto the old man, no longer feeling any trepidation about letting him into my home. Once the particulars were sorted, I said goodbye and headed back through the mall to find Zelda. I was halfway back to the atrium when a man jumped in front of me and stuck out his hands.

"You look like the kind of woman that reads a lot!" he said.

"Whatever you're selling, I'm not interested," I said as I side-stepped to move around him.

"That's just the thing!" he said, moving into a backwards jog while keeping up with me. "The only thing I'm selling is opportunity! The new Pear Dragon Tablet, the X100 Model! 250GB of space! Permanent internet connection! Yours for only $400!"

"Yeah, I've seen adverts for those stupid tablets everywhere, and to be honest I really don't have a need for one. So, bye!"

"You can download all of Wikipedia on this thing!" he shouted.

"I don't care!" I shouted back.

Managing to rid myself of the tablet salesman, I took the escalator back down to the atrium and found that Zelda was already waiting for me there.

"What do you think?" she asked as I approached. "Do they look okay?"

I had to get in really close and squint to inspect the work. I stepped back and tilted my head. "Have you had your appointment yet?"

"Yes! I just spent twenty minutes getting my brows done! You really can't tell?"

"I mean… maybe? They look almost exactly the same to be honest," I admitted.

"Then it's perfect."

"What?" I asked in confusion. "They *do* look the same."

Zelda put a hand on my shoulder and shook her head. "Maybe to the casual observer like you, but trust me, Will is definitely going to notice. He's always had a thing for my brows."

"If you say so…" I said with uncertainty as we started walking to the food court.

"So, how was your visit to the furniture restoration man?" Zelda asked, a fresh bounce in her step.

"Interesting to say the least. I thought he was a spy for the dark witches, but it turns out he's a divination magician. It felt quite unsettling until he did a reading for me."

"Yeah, I always feel sick around those guys. What did the reading say?"

"He said there are three traitors, and I figured there was just one."

Zelda scoffed. "So, we have to keep our eyes peeled for three potential traitors? Things are never simple with you, eh?"

"You're preaching to the choir sister."

After snacking at the food court, I dropped Zelda back at the café and I went home to my apartment. My first port of call was to check in with Fancy Bill, to see if he'd drawn up any interesting facts about knowledge demons yet.

"Wake up, you stupid skull," I said as I walked into the bakery pantry. Fancy Bill snored himself awake and his eyes ignited with blue flame.

"Ah, not the pony!" he screamed. I just stared at him for an awkward moment. "Oh, hi Zora."

"…Hi. Dreaming again?"

"Don't you worry about that. What can I help you with?"

"I wanted to know if you've figured out anything else about our knowledge demon?"

"Banging that drum again? I already told you, you're just going to have to wait this guy out."

"Unfortunately, that's not very helpful. I'm beginning to wonder how useful an 'all-knowing' creature is, when they don't know anything."

"Well, what do *you* know about this knowledge demon?" Fancy Bill asked.

"It's taken over the library, it eats books for knowledge, it turns people into statues if they get in its way… that's about the long and short of it."

"Run this 'book' thing by me again?" he said.

"I beg your pardon?"

"Book. What's this book thing again?"

"Seriously? How can you not know what a book is?"

"I mean I know what a book is, but there weren't a lot of them around when I last existed. The printing press was only invented in 1439, and I served Layla the Terrible from 1502 to 1512, you filthy stinking hobo!"

"Hey! Enough of the name calling. So, books weren't really all that common back then, huh?"

"Nope. Back then knowledge demons actually took over cloisters of monks. Most of the time they would absorb knowledge just by reading scrolls. To be honest the book eating is a new thing. It's a lazier way of absorbing the material."

I straightened up. "Wait a second. This demon doesn't actually have to eat books to absorb knowledge?"

"Nope. Why?"

My eyes opened wide as I happened upon a potential solution for the knowledge demon problem. "Fancy Bill, that's it! I could kiss you!"

"Oh my god, please keep your revolting flesh-covered skull away from me!" he gagged. I didn't hear whatever else he had to say because I ran back upstairs to my apartment.

Library tomorrow, I texted Zelda. *Figured out demon problem.*

A moment later Zelda messaged back. *Okay, whatevz!*

With a minor triumph achieved I showered, changed into my pajamas and got ready for bed. After a little light reading, I turned over to switch off the bedside light and screamed as I saw a ghost sitting next to the bed.

He was translucent blue and dressed the exact same as he always did when he was alive, his Yankees jersey shimmering away in its ghostly form.

"Dad?!"

"Hey baby!" he said warmly. "How's it going?!"

CHAPTER 13

"What are you—how are you—where did you—you're a ghost!" I sputtered, sitting up straight and staring at the ghost of my dead father.

He chuckled in his old familiar way, his eyes disappearing in a sea of warm crinkles. "Yeah, kind of cool, huh? It's been a few weird years, but I can't say it hasn't been interesting."

My dad died three years ago, meaning that he went out of my life before I had a chance to discover that I was a witch. I'd only gained the ability to see ghosts since inheriting my magic, the first one being my Aunt Constance when I moved to Compass Cove several months ago.

"I thought I'd never see you again," I choked, tears brimming in my eyes.

"Hey, hey, come on now," he said, floating on over and sitting beside me on the bed. He had no corporeal form, and instead of human warmth there was the strange chill one came to associate with spirits, but having him there next to me was still incredibly comforting. "There's no need to get upset. If you start the waterworks, then you just know that I'm going to start too. Don't go making me look bad!" he joked.

I laughed and wiped the tears away, noticing ghostly tears forming in his translucent blue eyes. "I'm sorry, you just caught me by surprise is all. It's... *so* good to see you," I said, letting out a very long breath. "You have no idea how much I've missed you."

"Well, I reckon I do, because I'm mighty happy to see you too. Truth is I've been looking for you for a while. When I died, I spent a lot of time around you making sure you were safe, or just watching you move through the world without me."

"Really?" I asked. "It always felt like you were near."

He nodded proudly. "Of course, I was. My body might have left the world, but I was still there to look after my Zora. I wasn't going to let anything happen to you. After a while though my mood started to change—I was upset a lot of the time. Sad that I couldn't speak to you, or have you see me, or even give me a hug! It was then that I noticed my presence was effecting your life negatively. That streak of hard luck you came upon? That was no coincidence, that was because old daddy was hanging around and messing things up for you by accident."

I wrinkled my nose and shook my head dismissively. "What? Daddy, no, that stuff wasn't your fault. Sometimes life just throws you a curveball. You taught me that."

"I did indeed. But it turns out it *was* my presence messing things up for you. I made a few friends on this side and they told me as much. An unhappy ghost can inadvertently pass bad energy onto humans around them. It was then that I realized I had to go and find some sort of peace before I came back to you again. So, I went on a trip with some ghost friends, and we spent some time travelling the states."

"Hey, you always wanted to do a big trip like that," I said, feeling so happy he'd finally got his chance—even if it *was* after death.

"Zora, I have to tell you, I've had the time of my life since becoming a ghost. I'll bring my friends over at some point too and introduce them to you. Anyway, after a few months I was feeling a lot better about myself, and I realized what was bringing me down. I decided to come back and check up on you. There was something I wanted to tell you, I just had to figure out how. But when I got back home, I realized you were gone. Packed up and left!"

"You must have come back after I'd moved across country to Compass Cove," I realized.

He nodded. "Yup, I think that's about what happened. I never was great with my timing. I knew your momma was a witch and she came from witch town, but she'd never given me anything else more specific than that. For a few moments I was distraught, convinced that I'd have to spend the rest of time looking for you, but one of my ghost friends taught me a way of finding people. If you're looking for someone your intuition will guide you—as a ghost anyway."

"So you came across the country to find me?" I asked.

"Yup. And as I travelled, I spoke to more ghosts along the way. Told them where I was going and who I was looking for. And would you believe it, about halfway across the country I found that ghosts started to know who you were. 'Zora Wick?' they'd say. 'The witch that solves murders! I've heard about her!' Well, as I got closer and closer, I met more folk that have heard of you. It seems you're the talk of the town!"

"The ghosts know who I am?" I said in confusion.

He nodded again. "Sure do! Apparently, some woman called 'Constance' has been singing your praises to just about every ghost that she comes across. You've become something of a celebrity amongst the dead, Z!" he said with a chuckle.

I couldn't help but smile as the puzzle pieces came together. It was quite sweet to hear that Constance had been blabbing about to me anyone she came across. "Constance is mom's sister, Dad." We both paused momentarily at mention of mom. "I've been trying to find out what happened to her actually. I thought she might be back here, but she disappeared not long after she got back. Do you know I've got a half-sister?"

"You do?" he said with surprise. "What's she like?"

"She's… my best friend."

A smile spread over his face. "I'm glad. I always wished I could have given you a sibling. I've been trying to find your mother too so I could speak with her again, but I can't feel any presence in my heart."

"So what was it you wanted to talk to me about?" I asked. "You mentioned there was something."

"That's right," he said, floating up from the bed and pacing across the room. "When I first died and spent that time watching you, my mood was in the wrong place because there was something I'd wanted to tell you, but never got the chance. I guess it was eating me up inside that I never got around to doing it."

"Okay..." I said slowly. "Why do I get the feeling this is a bad thing?"

"It's not a bad thing," he said assuredly. "The only bad thing is that I wish I told you earlier. And if you hate me for it that's okay. I'll float away and you won't have to see me again."

"Now you've really got me worried. Just spit it out already, I'm sure it's not that bad."

He took a very deep breath—more habitual than necessary—and rubbed his hands over his face. "Alright, here goes. Zora... I'm not your real father."

I did a double take. "Excuse me?"

"I'm not your real father. I'm the man that raised you, and I'll always call you my daughter, but the truth is that I'm not your biological dad."

The world seemed to fall apart in that moment. Waves of confusing emotion swept over me. The urge to cry bubbled up and threatened to spill, but I bit back the tears to get answers. "I don't understand. Who is my dad then?"

"I... I don't know," he said, scratching the back of his head. "It's part of the reason I wanted to track your momma down, so I could help you figure it out. But gosh darn it... she's as much as mystery in death as she was in life." Dad floated back over to the bed and put one of his icy hands on mine. "Darling, are you okay?"

"I think I'm just shocked," I said, blinking slowly as I tried to reconcile the truth. "So... how did you end up raising me? You and momma were together?"

"For a time," he admitted. "Though it was actually several years before you were born. We first met back in the seventies. After that we spent some time together on the hippie scene. We had a few good years. Eventually we went our separate ways. I grew up, got an office job and a mortgage, and one stormy night out of the blue your mother turned up, heavily pregnant. She was shaking, scared for her life, told me she had nowhere else to run.

"I took her in and told her everything was okay. She could have the baby here and I'd help her look after it. Well, you were born, a beautiful baby girl might I add, and I'd never seen your mother happier. The happiness didn't last long however, she told me she had to go, that it was the only way to keep you safe. I told her she didn't have to leave. Whatever it was we could handle it together, but she was adamant that staying would only put the three of us in danger."

"Did she mention what it was?"

He shook his head. "No, but I'd never seen her more afraid. I knew it had something to do with the magic world she was from, but we never really spoke about those things. She told me she couldn't say much about it. Since dying I've learned more about magic than when I was alive, but I still have no idea what she was running from. I understand if you hate me—"

"Hate you?" I blurted. "What on earth makes you think I hate you?"

"Zora, you deserved to know the truth a lot sooner. I shouldn't have waited as long as I did."

I put one of my hands on his cold ghostly form and smiled. "You know for a ghost that claims to have learned so much, you're still a big dummy." He laughed. "I'll admit it's one *heck* of a shock, but you're still my dad. I love you."

"I love you too," he said, looking relieved to finally have that weight off his shoulders.

"I'm trying to find out what happened to her actually. We think she might be trapped in something called the mirror dimension. I'm pretty sure I saw her hiding in the reflection of my mirror a few weeks ago."

Dad's brow knit together. "This magic business, it still confuses the heck out of me."

I laughed this time. "Hey, me too, and I'm the one that's supposed to be a witch. So, are you going to tell me about your travels then or what?"

"Now?" he said. "Darling I already felt bad enough dropping in this late. I literally just got into town, and I had to see you. Don't you need to sleep?"

"Eh, I'll sleep when I'm dead. Right now, the only thing I want to do is stay up and talk with you. I've missed you dad. I've missed you a lot."

"I've missed you too Zora, but I'm always there, watching over you." He paused and let the sweet moment linger between us for a few seconds. Then he took another deep breath and collected himself. "Now… you want to hear about my travels, eh. Let me ask you a question. Have you ever seen the world's biggest elastic ball?"

"No." I giggled. "Did you?"

"Sure did! And let me tell you… this thing was humongous. Now my friend Cal, that's one of my ghost pals I told you about, he said he saw a bigger one when he was in Germany, but if you told him you've been to Timbuktu, he'd say he's been to Timbukthree. One of them types, you know?"

"Oh, I've got a few of them in my life…" I laughed. I didn't look at the clock as we talked, I just sat there with my dad and we talked the hours away. I had my dad back again—I wasn't going to take that for granted.

CHAPTER 14

"Rise and shine!" Zelda bellowed. "I brought you a caramel Frappuccino!"

Without warning Zelda threw back the curtains, blinding wedges of sunlight pierced into my dark bedroom and thrust me from the deep throes of sleep.

"It burns, it burns!" I moaned melodramatically while throwing the covers back over my head.

"Ah you'll be fine." Zelda trudged over to the bed and threw the covers back. In a last ditch attempt I covered my head with the pillows until she threw these off too.

"Why are you doing this to me?" I groaned.

"Because you texted me last night to say that we were going to the library today. When I got to the bakery this morning Daphne and Rosie said you hadn't been downstairs yet, which is highly suspicious. You normally do the morning bake with them even when you're not on the schedule. Then I rang the apartment door and there was no answer—I had to use my spare key to get in!"

"You have a spare key?" I said groggily.

Zelda looked at me as though it was a stupid question. "Of course,

I do. I used to come here all the time and practice lines for my amateur dramatics class."

Actually, now that I thought about it, I already knew that. The first time I ever met Zelda I had barged into the bakery because I thought she was being attacked. It turned out she was just reading lines for a play. She never actually rehearsed for these parts on account of being chronically shy, and most of her interest in the local theatre stemmed from the fact that she had a crush on one of the guys there.

"But why the military wakeup call?" I groaned again while pushing myself up into a sitting position.

She laughed. "I'd hardly call nine in the morning a military wakeup call. Besides, I would have woken you up earlier, I was here at half after eight. I saw that you were still sleeping so I decided to go out and get you a nice drink. Voila!"

Zelda put the syrup-topped coffee into my hands, and I took it gratefully. "It is much appreciated, thank you." I took a long slurp of the sugary-sweet drink. A long yawn escaped me, and Zelda plonked herself down on the bed.

"So, are you going to tell me why you're so tired? Late night visit from Hudson?" Her brows danced in a suggestive way, and she nudged me with her elbow.

"Full disclosure, we do *not* have that kind of sisterly relationship," I said, feeling slightly nauseous just at the prospect of discussing my private life with Zelda.

She pulled back and balked at me in disgust. "Oh god, I don't want to actually hear anything about it! Why would you put that in my head?!"

"You're the one that brought it up, you nitwit! As it stands, I did have a late-night visitor actually. But it wasn't Hudson."

This time an expression of shock came over. "Zora! You're cheating on him!?" she said in a hushed whisper.

"No, you moron," I said swiping my hand at her. She ducked out of the way. "I was just about to turn the light off to go to sleep when I saw my dad's ghost sitting next to the bed."

"Your dad?" Zelda gasped. "Have you seen him since he died?"

"No, and it was quite lovely actually, we spent a lot of time catching up."

And so, I ended up catching Zelda up on the happenings with my dad. I wasn't sure what time I went to bed in the end, but the last time I looked at the clock it was after three in the morning. Dad left so I could get some sleep but mentioned on his way out that he'd be sticking around in Compass Cove for a while.

"That explains why you're so tired then," she said. "Did you have any idea he wasn't your real dad before last night?"

"No, not at all. It came as a bit of a shock to be honest, but I don't think it changes anything between us."

"Now you have to find out why mom disappeared, *and* who your real dad is. The mysteries never stop piling up with you, eh?"

"Yes, I'm so blessed. Anyway, let me get ready quickly and then we can head out to the library. I know how to deal with the book demon problem—I think. We need to go to the mall first though."

"The mall? Why?"

"Ah, ah, a good magician never reveals her secrets."

Zelda skipped out of the room, and I decided to wear the previous day's outfit to avoid getting any more hassle from Constance's magic wardrobe. After dressing, I stepped out of my bedroom and Zelda came around the corner, holding a hand over her mouth as she rushed for the bathroom. "There's a... man... at the door. Says he's here to see your..." With that she took off to the bathroom, shut the door and I heard the muted sound of vomiting.

How pleasant.

As I walked into the apartment I saw Chang, the old Asian man from the furniture restoration place, waiting in the front door. "Sorry about that, do come on in," I said and went over to close the door behind him. I noticed I no longer had the nauseous feeling around him, that reading really had done wonders.

"It's okay, I am quite used to the reaction. I will see to the wardrobe and be out of your hair. Where is she?"

"Through here, follow me this way."

I led Chang into Constance's bedroom and pointed at the magical wardrobe. Chang looked around with unease at the Donny Osmond pictures and smiled at me nervously. I guess it was his turn to feel uncomfortable for once. "I forgot about this room..." he grimaced, looking at the pictures covering every surface. "I had hoped I might never come back.

"Quite unnerving, isn't it? How long will this take? It's just that we're heading out."

"About an hour or two. I can come another day if this morning doesn't work?"

"No, that's fine. I don't want to be an inconvenience. Just let yourself out once the work is done. Help yourself to anything in the kitchen."

"That is very kind, but I will pass. The western diet is not to my taste. I will come back when you are less busy," Chang picked up his toolbox and made to leave.

"I have no problem with you staying while we're out!" I said, hastily following him.

"I mean no inconvenience by it. It is best for a divination magician to not be in an abode without the owner or a resident present. We can inadvertently mess with the energy otherwise."

But I really wanted this wardrobe issue fixing. "Uh... uh... what about my familiar?!" I said, yanking Hermes up by the scruff of his neck and holding him up high. He was still sleeping. "He can watch you?"

Hermes opened one sleepy eye. "Huh?"

Chang stopped and turned back to face me. "A familiar will work, yes. He will need to remain in the room with me however."

"Hey, if it's familiars you want, I've got them in spades. There's a time owl over there, and there's even an oracle in the pantry."

"My," Chang said, taken aback. "Quite the collection you have there. May I see the time owl?"

I took Chang over to Phoebe, who, like Hermes, spent ninety percent of her time asleep. "Phoebe, wake up and do something interesting," I said, prodding her.

The owl opened her eyes one at a time and narrowed them at me. "Tomorrow it will be Wednesday."

"See?" I said to Chang. "She can even see into the future. Just like you." I was mostly being sarcastic because Phoebe was utterly useless for the most part, but as I turned around to look at Chang, I noticed he was on all fours with his arms pressed against the ground. "Uh…"

"It's about time I got some recognition around here," Phoebe said.

"Oh, great and powerful time owl!" Chang said. "Forgive the absence of my gift. If I had known that one such as you resided here, I would have prepared one!"

Phoebe blinked, her eyes not quite in sequence, and then she yawned. "Okay, no big deal."

Chang jumped back onto his feet, looking a lot more nervous now. "I'm sorry Miss Wick, you did not mention I would be in the presence of such a divine creature!"

"Don't sweat it, most of the time she's just a lazy rainbow-colored owl," I said.

"Pot kettle black," Phoebe replied without looking directly at me.

"Divination magicians freaking worship these guys," Hermes muttered to me. He was still in my arms and had woken up properly now. Needless to say, I was kind of picking up on that vibe.

I momentarily left Chang to admire Phoebe, while I took Hermes back to the kitchen and set him on the counter. "Well, he's here to service Constance's wardrobe. Can you keep an eye on him? He says he can't work unless there are residents present."

"I'll do it, but it's going to cost you. Ten tins of that extra fancy cat food."

"Fine, whatever." I already had some in the cupboard anyway.

"And I want daily massages, lasting a *minimum* of three hours," he said, perhaps sensing that his initial demand wasn't that much of a win.

"Um, how about no?" I said and scratched his head. Zelda came out of the bathroom looking paler than usual. "Ah, there you are. Let's get going then. We've got wrongs to right and mysteries to crack open."

Zelda hurried towards the front door, trying her best to stay clear

A SCONE TO PICK

of Chang, who was still worshipping the time owl. "Is it just me or is the room spinning?" she asked.

"That's the room. I set it to spin. Should I turn it off?" I joked, holding the door open for her.

"You won't be laughing when I throw up on your stairs."

"I will be when I watch you clean it up."

We successfully navigated our way to the mall without Zelda throwing up anymore. As we pulled into the parking lot, I noticed that her skin still looked grey and clammy, like some sort of sick frog, so I took her to the food court for a snack and she perked right up.

"So, where are we going?" Zelda said cheerily.

"Right this way," I said, steering her towards the store for the expensive tablets.

"The Pear Dragon store?" she scoffed. "This stuff is very overpriced." Her eyes glossed over as we walked past a display stand of shiny metallic laptops sporting the Pear Dragon logo. Zelda veered off towards the display, her voice taking on a more hypnotic quality. "But also so beautiful…"

I left Zelda to fall into the clutches of capitalism and wandered over to the tablet display. I'd barely been there three seconds when the salesman from the day before approached me with his predatory grin.

"Let me guess, you've been up all-night thinking about it."

"Not exactly, how much for this hunk of junk again?"

"The X100 Model? 250gb of space. Permanent internet connection. Yours for only $400!"

Yikes. Not exactly pocket change. With a regretful sigh I pulled out my purse and grabbed my card. "Here's hoping this works. What's your returns policy by the way?"

"There's a three-day grace period, in that time items can be returned for store credit."

"Man, you guys really went and redefined cutthroat, huh?" I said.

"I beg your pardon?" the salesman asked, his smile faltering a little.

"Nothing, just ring it up."

Fifteen minutes later Zelda and I left the expensive tech store, me with my tablet and Zelda with her $2000 laptop computer. "The best part is the 8k quantum display!" she said excitedly. "That's like… much more than my other computer! There's also 32gb of RAM!"

"What's RAM?" I asked her. I mean, I knew the answer, I did a stint one summer working in a computer shop, but I was fairly confident that Zelda didn't.

"I don't know, but the sales guy said it was good. And look how pretty this thing is. They've got a zero-credit payment plan and everything, and he said I can run Hamster Grape Kingdom no problem!"

If I had a drink, I would have spit it out at that point. Zelda was just *slightly* obsessed with a very simple browser game called Hamster Grape Kingdom, a game where two-dimensional cartoon hamsters had to sort falling grapes into rows of three to clear a board.

"Are you going to tell me what the tablet is for anyway?" she asked as we climbed into the car.

"This little bad boy," I said, unboxing it and beginning to set it up. "Is going to get us back our library."

"How on earth are you going to defeat an army of demons with an over-priced tablet? I mean—a very pretty one at that."

"You'll see," I said with a grin on my face. "I've got a plan."

"And I've got a super pretty laptop! We're both winners!"

"I'm not sure our credit scores would agree with that one."

"Shh!" Zelda hissed, stroking the laptop box like it was a puppy. "We don't speak about bad things like that around the pretty gadgets."

"Come on," I said, putting the van into gear and backing out of the spot. "It's time we got our library back."

CHAPTER 15

"Tony! Tony!" the imp greeted us as we approached the entrance to the magic library. There was no need to blast open the spiral staircase this time, the nailed-down boards automatically opened on our approach, and our familiar imp friend popped out in his designer Italian suit. "What brings you back to the domain of Big Tony?"

"Actually, Tony, we came to make a peace offering. I have a gift here in this tote bag, one that I believe will make Big Tony leave this library and return it to us."

The little red imp doubled over with laughter. "Oh, you're being serious? Well, okay, let's have a look in the bag then. I needs to make sure you witch broads ain't trying to sneak any weapons in here."

After opening the tote bag and showing him the tablet the imp gave me a rather confused look. "What is that? Some sort of tabletop?"

Zelda squinted at the imp currently guarding the staircase. "Aren't you guys knowledge demons? You don't know what a tablet is?"

"Hey lady we just eat the knowledge. No one said anything about us being smart, okay? Not that I'd expect you numb nuts to understand, but knowledge is our food, capeesh?"

"Bada Bing, Bada boom," Zelda responded.

"What?" the imp growled.

"I just figured I'd join in with the made-up sounds."

"So," I cut in. "Can we see Big Tony? I promise he's going to like it."

"I don't see why not," the imp said, passing his hands over the outside of the bag like an airport scanner. "Doesn't feel like a hidden magic weapon to me, so I'll give you the greenlight. Follow me! Uh, word to the wise though, he's most likely just going to turn you into a statue."

"Nah," I said dismissively, "I'm pretty sure we don't have to worry about that."

And so, we followed the imp and made our way through the magic library, hearing the name 'Tony' countless times along the way. After ten minutes of walking, we reached the impromptu castle made of books, and our escort led us into the main chamber with Big Tony. The large demon was sitting atop his throne, shoveling books into his face while his never-ending stream of servants came through the room with more offerings.

"Oh, look who's back," said Big Tony, his deep voice sounding irritated and disinterred. "Alright, pick your poses."

"Poses?" I asked.

"I told you what would happen if you came back here, you can join your friends at the back of the room and be statues for the rest of the eternity. Now pick a good pose. There's no changing it," he warned.

"Actually, we came here to bring you something, an offering."

"Pass!" the large demon belched. Without warning he snapped his fingers in my direction and a glittering bolt of green magic shot my way. "Statue time!"

To be honest I anticipated that the large demon would at least want to see what we'd brought first, but luckily enough I was quick to react and pulled my wand out. I had no time to think of a spell incantation, so I just mentally urged the thought of a protective orb around me and Zelda.

His attack spell hit, just as a huge iridescent golden sphere of light surrounded Zelda and me. The glittering green bolt disintegrated harmlessly and every creature in the room stopped and looked our way.

"...Woah," Tony, our escorting imp, said slowly.

To my surprise Big Tony started laughing. As he did so the rest of his imp minions joined in until he abruptly stopped and silenced them. He then put down a pile of books he was about to drop into his mouth, leaned forward on the chair and steepled his sofa-sized fingers. "So, you ain't no ordinary witches, huh? It takes a broad with pretty big balls to march in here and knock back demon magic like it ain't no trouble."

"Isn't," I corrected. "Isn't no trouble. I'm sorry, but it's really doing my head in. And also, what's the big deal? It's just a magic shield," I said, staring through the golden forcefield as I maintained eye contact with the big bad.

"Just a shield?" the big demon said. "Just a shield!" Once again, he threw his head back and laughed, and the rest of his minions started laughing too until their master stopped. "Silence!" he barked at them, turning his attention on us once more.

"Zora, blocking demon magic is pretty huge," Zelda murmured in my ear. "Their magic is normally far more powerful than ours. I don't know what spell you cast here to protect us, but it has to be seriously powerful."

"I just thought up a quick protective spell," I said with a shrug. "No big deal."

"Eh, it's a pretty big deal lady," the staircase imp said to our right. "Safe to say you have Big Tony's attention now."

I looked back at the giant demon and noticed he was staring at us with expectation. "Well," he prompted. "Go on then, the floor is yours. It's your turn to attack me."

"I... beg your pardon?" I said in confusion.

"You might think us demons to be wild and uncouth," the staircase imp said, "but when it comes to magical combat, we have a code of conduct that we uphold with enemies that we respect. All magical duels consist of taking turns. He attacked, you defended. Now it's your turn to attack."

"That's *almost* civilized of you," Zelda pointed out.

"Hey, it's only because he respects that there magical shield you just threw up. Keep wasting time though and the privilege of respect will quickly fall to the wayside."

"I'm getting bored…" the large demon said, rapping the fingers of one hand on his book throne.

"Quick Zora, smoke him!" Zelda said. I looked at my sister and Big Tony and rolled my eyes. With a swish of my hand, I dispelled the magical shield and took a few steps forward. "Don't take down the shield!" Zelda hissed.

"Oh relax," I said, continuing to walk forward. I'd already proved that I could handle whatever this big guy had to throw at me, and I wanted to show that I wasn't afraid, and that I didn't come here to fight. With my tote bag on my shoulder, I approached the book throne and stopped a few feet short of it. Big Tony actually looked a little nervous as I got closer.

"That's close enough," he gulped. "I've got other spells. Dangerous ones. I'll use them!"

"Shut up, you big idiot," I sighed, reading his very obvious bluff. "In this bag I have a gift for you. It contains infinite knowledge. I will give it to you on the condition that you return this library, repair the damage you have done, unfreeze my friends and vow to never steal another witch library again."

"Ha! And why would I do that?" he scoffed.

I pulled the little tablet out of my bag and held it up in the air. "Because I have this."

"What is that?" he said, leaning in closer to get a better look. "Some sort of miniature tabletop?"

"It's a tablet, with a permanent internet connection. Do you know what the internet is?"

"…Yes," Big Tony said uncertainly.

"What is it?" I asked.

"It's like a series of tubes, and there's this big truck—"

"Stop right there. The internet is a place chock full of information. See this video site? There are 30,000 hours of footage uploaded by

A SCONE TO PICK

people every *hour*. This website? It's an infinite encyclopedia maintained by thousands of editors... for free! Then there's memes, and clickbait, social media, not to mention all the other stuff!"

Big Tony stared at me for a very long moment. "Wait a second... 30,000 hours of footage an hour?"

"Yup," I said. "And some of it's even pretty good. You can learn anything you want on the internet, and you can do it all from the palm of your hand with this little beauty."

At that moment something unexpected happened, Big Tony slipped a ring off his finger and shrank down to the size of one of the normal minions. The large horns on his head were apparently fake, because he slipped them off and set them down.

"Tony! Put the ring back on!" one of the other Tony's said disparagingly. "You're ruining the illusion!"

"Shut up you moron!" Not so Big Tony shouted back. "This witch comes here with her high-level spells and an electronic tabletop containing infinite knowledge! She can see through the veil!"

"It's called a tablet," I corrected, fruitlessly.

"Yes, yes," he said quickly. "What are your terms again? What do I have to do to obtain this fountain of power?" he said, his eyes fixed upon the tablet.

"Unfreeze my friends, restore and return the library, never steal a witch library again."

"...We have a deal," Big Tony said, still staring at the device. He pulled his attention away momentarily and shouted to the minions. "Alright boys, put everything back and tidy up! We leave in the hour!" With that order, the army of imp minions started hurrying about again in every direction, dismantling the book fortress around us with alarming speed.

"One hour?" I said. "I want everything restoring back to normal. This isn't a rush job."

"Relax Tony," Big Tony said. "My boys work fast." He made hand pistols and shot magic at the statues behind us, returning our friends back to normal. The frozen library staff all looked around the room in confusion. Agnes, the old witch with the appearance of a five-year-old girl, stormed over to us with fury upon her face.

"I told you you'd regret messing with this place!" she barked, jabbing a finger at the knowledge demon. A smile came over her as she turned her attention on me. "Zora, so nice to see you. Zelda, you too. What's going on?"

"They're leaving and restoring all the damage. They'll be done and gone in an hour." I looked back at 'Big' Tony and passed him the tote bag with the tablet and its instructions. "Make sure you read the manual," I said, "And make sure you thoroughly research 'critical thinking' before you let yourself loose on there." The last thing I needed was an army of imps falling down the conspiracy rabbit hole of the internet.

"Critical thinking, got it," Big Tony said as he slung the tote bag over his shoulder. "What do you want in return for the infinite tabletop?"

"It's called a—you know what, never mind. I don't need anything in return, we already made our deal."

"Actually Zora, knowledge demons have a culture of fair exchange when it comes to transacting physical goods," Agnes put in.

"Between that and the fighting you guys almost do seem civilized," I said to Big Tony. It was just a shame about the library stealing and turning people in statues.

"What do you want then, Zora Wick, grand master of magic and knowledge?"

I scoffed at the title. "Uh... I don't know dude. Whatever you think is a fair exchange for the tablet. To be honest you can get them from any shop for a few hundred dollars."

"That may be so, but you will forever be the person that first passed on the gift of infinite knowledge to us, so..." Big Tony eyed up the ring in his palm and handed it to me. "Have this, it's one of our most valuable treasures, it's a ring of enlarging. It used to be cursed, but I ate the curse."

Agnes blinked at the gift. "Woah, that's a... pretty significant gift Zora. In exchange for a tablet too? Not bad, not bad at all."

"Take this too," Big Tony said, fishing something else out of his pocket. He handed me a small black metal cube with intricate carvings on each side.

"Uh thanks…" I said. "Paperweight, right?"

"It's a pandora box," he said casually, turning the tablet over in his hands and admiring the glossy screen. "You can trap pretty much any entity you like in that thing, and they won't be able to get out."

From the look on Agnes and Zelda's faces I could tell this was apparently an item of extreme significance. "Thanks," I said. The ring alone felt like a fair trade.

"And I guess we're in your debt," Big Tony mumbled under his breath.

"Pardon?"

The demon looked uncomfortable for some reason. "Just… just forget about it? Okay? If you find yourself in any trouble just know that Big Tony and the boys have got your back."

"Oh, okay. Thanks for your generosity," I said. "The library was all I wanted though, really."

"Here's something you might not know about us knowledge demons Tony, get on our good side and we are very generous beings. Now if you'll excuse me, I have to go and start catching up on some internet. Think I can get up to date in 200 years?"

"Sure," I said, though something told me the knowledge demon problem had been taken care of for the foreseeable future. As Big Tony walked away, Zelda and I turned to face Agnes.

"Well then, you only went and did it," Agnes said, looking rather impressed. "I'll have to spread the word and let other witch libraries out there know that knowledge demons are hot for tablets. And Zelda, consider yourself bumped back up. You're now an Emerald-level bookworm."

"Yes!" Zelda said, pumping her fist in the air and drawing it back down again slowly.

"What is this thing anyway?" I said, putting the pandora box into my bag.

"Both of those items are very powerful demon artifacts. Demons don't just go around giving those out for free you know?" Agnes said. "The ring in itself is extremely powerful, but the box... I've read about them in books. You can use them to trap powerful entities."

"Any other place on earth I'd wonder how useful that might be," I said. This was Compass Cove however, and trouble was as reliable as the rain. "This ring is safe to use?"

"A knowledge demon won't lie once you're on his side, and after your gift it sounds like he's definitely on your side. Try it on, if there's any trouble Jake will take care of it, he's good with curses. Except for mine of course." Agnes thumbed to Jake, who was still standing on the opposite side of the room. The silent twelve-foot giant was a jackal-headed Anubis who acted as Agnes' assistant.

I slipped the ring on and all of a sudden, I grew in size, the floor beneath me rapidly shrinking away as my head neared the tall ceiling of the book fortress. I had to be at least twenty feet tall now. "Woah! This is amazing!" I shouted, my voice booming all around me. I took the ring off again and returned to normal size. I slipped the magical trinket into my pocket and smiled. "Remind me not to use that one inside."

"Well then, I do believe *I* owe you something as well Zora Wick," Agnes said to me. "I asked you to help me with my library problem, and sure enough you did. In exchange I grant you access to the restricted section—with my guidance of course. You were looking into your mother, right?"

"That's right," I said. "I want to see the last few books she had on the mirror dimension and—" Just then my phone started ringing in my pocket, it was Sheriff Burt. "One second, I have to take this."

"Wick, where the heck are you? I've been trying to get hold of you all morning!" Burt said.

"Sorry Burt, I'm at the... library."

"Well get your nose out of whatever book it's in and come down to the station. Wayne and Zayne picked up the runaway fiancé this morning."

"You found Howard Price? Where was he?"

"Caught him heading back to his house, would you believe it. I stationed Wayne on watch there after you told me about the fiancé going missing. I figured it was a little suspicious, so… I guess the case is open again. Now get down to the station and help us question him, before his lawyer gets here!"

"Alright, I'll be right there." I put my phone away and looked at Agnes. "Sorry Agnes, my journey into the forbidden section will have to wait for now. There's been a break in a case I'm working on, and the police need my help."

It had been a busy morning of—literally—conquering demons. Now it seemed I had an afternoon of interrogation lined up. How hard could that be in comparison?

CHAPTER 16

"Ah, Zora Wick!" Linda Combs said delightedly as I walked into the police station. "Just the person I wanted to see! Now I've—"

"Linda, I regret to tell you that our crossword solving relationship has come to an end," I announced. "Please forward all future queries to your nearest search engine," I said, walking past her desk and towards the interview rooms.

"You—you can't do this!" she gasped. "I need your help! Using the computer is cheating!"

"Using me is cheating too!" I shouted as I turned around the corner and out of eyesight.

On the way to the room, I pulled out my phone and called Tamara Banana, the town's sole CSI, she answered after a few rings.

"Hey Zora, what's up?" she asked.

"Did you find anything else of interest at the crime scene? Any prints on the murder weapon?"

"No prints. I've sent that pollen sample off to a lab in Virginia, but I've not had anything back yet."

"Rats, that's what I was hoping for actually. I'm about to meet with

Helen Bowen's fiancé and he's a florist. It would have been handy to have an id on that pollen."

"Oh, well I can tell you what it's not—whatever flower that pollen came from, it's not a garden variety flower or a wildflower found in the continental united states."

"How do you know?" I asked.

"I have a limited local database in my lab that I can compare the sample to, and it doesn't match anything from our country."

"But this guy is a florist, he'll have flowers shipped in from all over the world, right?"

"And hasn't he been missing for several days?" she asked. "If you ask me, it looks very suspicious. Anyway, I'll give you a call when I get those results back. Good luck with your interrogation!"

I put my phone back into my pocket and as I rounded the corner, I saw Sheriff Burt approaching the interview room from the other end of the corridor. "Ah Wick, there you are. What do you say we sit down and talk to this guy together?" he said, stroking his silver moustache.

"Sure. What made you change your mind about the case then?" Last time we'd talked Burt was quite adamant the case was closed.

"Well you said it yourself, it's mighty suspicious this fella taking off. Let me make one thing clear I still think our man in the cell is responsible for this."

"Saxophone Joe," I clarified.

"Yes. My new angle is this—what if the hobo and the fiancé did this together somehow?"

I squinted at Burt. "Uh... what?"

He batted the idea away and chuckled to himself. "Eh, I guess we'll see. You take charge in there Wick. I'll chip in when I feel the need."

We went into the room and joined Howard Price at the brushed metal table. He was on the skinnier side, with large glasses, slicked back hair and a light brush of salt and pepper stubble upon his face.

"Howard Price, this here is Zora Wick. She's one of our independent investigators on this case. She'll be handling this talk," Burt said as an introductory manner.

Howard, wringing his hands together, sat up straight and readied himself. "Absolutely. Anything I can do to help."

"Can you tell us where you've been the last few days?" I asked him. "Your fiancée is murdered and then you take off into the wilderness without warning—you have to understand how incredibly suspicious that looks."

"Right, right," Howard fumbled. He laughed nervously and looked at the both of us. "Helen and I had a trip planned, we do it every year, a camping trip up to Lost Lovers Lake."

"A camping trip?" Burt said, leaning in as if to hear him better.

"That's right, we do it every year. We were supposed to leave the day after Helen died. When the officer came to my house and delivered the news I obviously broke down in disbelief, I had no intention of doing the trip after that."

"But you went anyway," I pointed out.

Howard wiped his nose on the sleeve of his rolled-up shirt collar and nodded. "Well, yes, this is going to sound crazy, but I had a dream that night—it was Helen telling me to take the trip. When I woke up in the morning, I swear I could feel her there next to me, urging me to go. I called and cleared it with someone at the station before leaving. Helen and I always turned our phones off on the trip, so I'd be unreachable for a few days."

Burt and I looked at one another. "I'm sorry," I said, "you left a message for someone at the station?"

"Yes, I called the officer who came to my house the night of her murder. He left me a business card. Officer Combs, I believe? I told him I'd be at Lovers Lake for two nights."

"Who went over to the house?" I said to Burt.

"It was Zayne," he said with a loaded sigh. "Do me a favor, Wick, go and speak with him, see if there's a message on the machine. I'd do it myself, but I can already see myself giving that boy a good whooping, and I ain't go the energy for it this morning. Take a left, third door on the right."

I swiftly exited the interview room and found Zayne asleep at his desk. I picked up a stack of paperwork on the desk and dropped it down again so the thud would wake him.

"Stop right there!" he shouted, waking with a jolt. After a second of confusion, he rubbed his eyes and looked at me. "Wick, what the heck do you want?"

"Our man in the interview room says he left a message on *your* machine. Do you have any messages?" Zayne's desk was cluttered with reams of paperwork and trash, so much of it that I couldn't even see a phone.

"Phone... phone..." he said, pouring through the sea of trash and letting it fall freely onto the floor. "Ah! Here it is!" Zayne pulled the phone out from underneath a phonebook. The number '78' flashed on the handset's screen in bright red numbers. Zayne saw the number and looked at me sheepishly. "There's a chance I might have accidentally set the ring to silent..." he admitted.

"You think so, idiot?" I scalded. I grabbed the phone off Zayne, turned the ringer back up and scanned through the voicemail messages until, sure enough, I found Howard's message.

"Hey there Officer Combs, this is Howard Price, we spoke last night. Helen and I had a trip planned to Lost Lover's lake, we do it every year, and... well I feel like she wants me to go, so I'm going to. If y'all need to reach me, I'll be up there. I just need to get away and clear my head, sorry."

Zayne opened his eyes wide and sat up straight in the chair. "Well, I'll be a skunk's uncle! He didn't do a runner! He even told us where he was going!"

I stared at Zayne, wondering how one person could be so bad at their job. "You need to clean up your desk and start acting like an actual policeman," I said. "This..." I pointed to his up-turned office. "This is a joke!"

"I'll get right on it, Miss Wick!" Zayne scrambled as I walked out of the office. I headed back to the interview room and joined Howard and Burt at the table.

"The story checks out," I said as I sat down. I looked at Burt. "Zayne's organizational skills however..."

Burt nodded as though he already knew. "I'll talk with him, I promise. Now, where were we?"

"I uh... went up to the lake for two days, and then when I got back, well—y'all arrested me outside the house," Howard recapped.

"Also found a vespa in his garage," Burt pointed out. "You know, those little Italian motorbikes?"

"Yes... I know what a vespa is Burt, thanks." I looked at Burt. "You ride?" I asked, recalling the motorcycle tracks found departing from the crime scene.

Howard nodded. "I use it to get to and from the flower shop. We use it for deliveries too. The customers love it."

"According to the secretary in Helen's office you came to visit her on the evening of her death. She overheard the two of you arguing?"

"Ah, yes," Howard admitted regretfully. "We've been having money problems recently and things have been a little tight."

"Care to elaborate on that one?" Burt probed.

"These last few years we've both been doing well, and as such our spending has expanded in accordance with our income. But recently business at the flower shop has slowed, and Helen doesn't get as many court referrals as she used to. Our income has dropped, but we didn't adjust the spending, we kind of assumed it would right itself."

"But it didn't," I concluded naturally.

"We've got debt that we need to sort out, but we're working on it," he said, scratching the back of his head nervously.

"And what prompted the argument?" Burt asked.

"We've both been stressed about money lately, as a surprise I thought it would be nice to arrange something to cheer Helen up. I booked a cruise. I went over the office to tell her about it because she'd had a hard day at work. I thought she'd be happy, but it ended up turning into a big argument. In retrospect I can see that the cruise was a bad idea—we're still paying off debts... I shouldn't have dropped several thousand on another holiday."

"The secretary said she heard you both shouting?" I commented.

He nodded. "Yes, I suppose there was a bit of back and forth. At the time I was upset she couldn't see the gesture for what it was, and she was upset I'd spent more money that we couldn't afford."

"Must have made you feel pretty stupid?" Burt suggested. "Maybe even make you angry enough to go home and come back so you could get the final word."

Howard stared at Burt as though he was mad. "No, not at all. Although we argued we left on pretty good terms. In the end I agreed the cruise was a bad idea, so I said I'd cancel it. I'd only lose a $200 holding fee. We both apologized to one another, and Helen said she'd be home soon."

"Do you mind if we could get a handwriting sample?" I said to Howard. "It's part of the investigation."

"Of course. Look, I understand that I'm a suspect. The partner always is, right? But I promise you, I'd never hurt a hair on Helen's head. I'm not a violent person. You can ask anyone."

"We appreciate the input," Burt said. "Give us two minutes, we're just going to have a sidebar." Burt stood up and gestured for me to follow him. We went into the hall and closed the door to the room.

"What's up?" I asked.

"It was him, he did it."

"What?" I laughed. "How did you reach that conclusion?"

"Call it instinct, Wick. Trust me, twenty years on this job and you have a knack for telling when people are lying."

"What's he lying about?"

"Oh, everything. As far as I'm concerned, the fiancé did it, and that hobo was involved somehow as well. Look at the facts, pollen was found at the murder scene, and he's a *florist*. There were motorbike tracks found leading away from the scene, and he uses a vespa to get to work and make flower deliveries."

"What about the murder weapon though? A chisel? We have no way of tracing that back to him."

"Maybe not, but I say we ask him if we can look around his place. Compare the tracks on the vespa to those left at the scene, and maybe see if a chisel is missing from whatever tools he might have lying around the house."

"Let's get this handwriting sample sorted first. I need to establish if Howard was the one that left the threatening note on Helen's car."

We headed back inside the room and joined Howard at the table. I read aloud the clipping from the news article containing the word cemetery, and had Howard write it back onto a piece of paper.

Once we were done, I thanked Howard, took the sample and looked at it, comparing it to the picture of the note left on Helen's car. Not only did the samples not match, but Howard had spelled cemetery correctly, ruling him out as the person behind the anonymous threat.

"What are you looking for exactly?" he asked me.

"Don't you worry yourself about that," Burt interjected. "By the way Howard, we were wondering if we could take a look around your house. Standard procedure of course."

"Of course," Howard stammered. "Can I tidy up first?"

Burt grinned. "Not exactly, friend. How about we take a trip over there now?"

"Sure," he said, looking a little unsettled by the idea.

"Before we end this, do you have any idea who might have wanted to hurt Helen?" I asked Howard.

"That's what I've been asking myself over and over," he said, holding his head in both his hands. "I told that Officer Combs I never trusted that Glen guy, but apart from that—"

"Glen guy?" I interrupted.

"Yeah," Howard said, lifting his head up. "He's been one of Helen's best friends since they were kids. I've met him a few times, and was always polite on the surface, but... I don't know, something about him just doesn't feel right. He's always been sort of obsessed with Helen."

"You passed this tip on to Officer Combs on the night of Helen's murder?" I asked.

He nodded. "Yeah. Didn't he relay that to you guys?"

Burt gave me a knowing look and rolled his eyes. "We'll check him out. What's his name?"

"Glen. Glen Atkins. He lives here in town."

Burt scribbled down the name. "Great, I'll be sure to look into that.

Now, we'll get a coffee and then go over to your place Mr. Price. Do you want anything?"

Howard shook his head. "No, no thanks."

"Alrighty then. Back in a few minutes." Burt left the room and I followed him once more.

"I'm liking this, Wick. All we have to do is match the vespa prints to the tracks at the crime scene, find proof of a missing chisel and boom! Case closed," Burt said, clapping his hands together heartily while we walked down the corridor.

"If it's alright with you I'm going to sit out of the house search," I said.

"Not interested?" Burt asked, looking a little surprised.

"No, not really. You don't need me there to match tire prints and look through a toolbox, unless I'm sorely mistaken."

"Fair enough, Wick, I think you're right about that. Your billable hours end here though for the day, you know that right?"

I could only find myself staring at Burt. I don't know how many times I had to explain that I wasn't doing this for the money. "Yes, thanks for reminding me, Burt. It stings, but I'm sure that somehow, I'll pull through," I said sarcastically and began to walk away.

I had plenty of other things to keep me busy while Burt and his boys looked into Howard and ruled him out properly. It was time to get to the library and find out what happened to mom.

CHAPTER 17

"Hold onto your pants," Agnes said as one of the flying wooden platforms took off from the ground and soared across the library. The Magic Library was so large that these flying platforms were necessary if you wanted to get anywhere on time.

Even though I'd only fixed the library problem yesterday, Big Tony and his imps had done a sterling job of cleaning the place up and getting it back to normal. You wouldn't have known anything had ever been different if you didn't know about the temporary demon takeover.

"They did a good job fixing up the place," I remarked to Agnes as we held on tight to the handrails of the flying wooden platform. We were racing towards the forbidden section, accessed through two goliath doors that were so large they nearly reached the library's ceiling.

"Did they?" Agnes said sarcastically. "That giant lump ate through .038% of our inventory! Those are books we're never going to get back!"

I had to admit I hadn't actually taken that into consideration when making my deal with Big Tony. "Was there anything valuable?"

"To be honest a lot of it was rubbish that needed clearing out anyway, but I'm still mad about it! Nothing truly valuable though. Those knowledge demons tend to grab hold of the first thing they find, luckily for me they set up their base of operations in the section of the library that covers magical tax laws."

"So absolutely nothing of value there was lost then," I said with a chuckle.

Agnes looked annoyed about it but amused at the same time. "Yes, things could have been a lot worse, put it that way."

After a few minutes of flying, the rapid wooden platform reached the large doors that gave entrance to the forbidden section. Instead of opening fully, there was a small entrance door near the top, sort of like a cat flap but for humans. We soared through the entrance and suddenly found ourselves in the dark and murky chambers of the forbidden section.

"Where are we going exactly?" the little metal moon face on the wooden platform asked us. Each platform had one of these personas, and this one was rather prone to yawning and appearing very bored by everything.

"Books about the mirror dimension," Agnes snipped. "I told you once already."

"It's not my fault your voice is extremely tiring," the platform responded drolly. Agnes just rolled her eyes and bit her tongue.

I wasn't really sure why the forbidden section had to look the way it looked. The chambers were dark, murky, and the thick mist reduced the surrounding bookshelves to mere shadows, making them look like dark outlines of waiting giants.

Suffice to say the place creeped the heck out of me.

"Why is it so weird in here?" I asked Agnes. "Can't you install a light or two?"

"This is just how she likes it," Agnes responded cryptically.

"Who sorry?"

"Hela, she's the one that looks after this place. If we're lucky we'll never run into her. It's been several happy decades since I had the misfortune of last seeing her."

"I thought you were the head librarian?" I asked her as the wooden platform began to slow down and lowered itself to the ground. The wooden gate popped open, and we both stepped onto the ground, mist swirling around our feet. Despite looking like a five-year-old girl Agnes was actually well into her eighties. She'd been hit with a permanent curse by her ex-husband, one that meant she got a little younger every time she cursed.

"Stay here, don't go anywhere," Agnes instructed the wooden platform.

"Would it kill you to say please?" the platform said snootily.

"*Please* shut up," Agnes sighed, and we began walking towards the nearest shelf.

"Well?" I asked, hurrying up so I could stay close to her. Everything about the forbidden section creeped me out, and as I caught up to her I found myself looking over my shoulder several times.

"Well, what?" she asked, looking spooked herself to be here.

"I thought you said you were the head librarian, but now you tell me someone else is in charge of the forbidden section?" I asked.

"Yes, Hela. She's a... ah, how do I put this? We needed someone powerful to make sure these books would be safe. There were several applicants for the job, but Hela in particular stood out. Let's just say she's tenacious in her ability."

"She's a witch?" I asked, trying to get a clarifying picture on this mysterious figure.

"She's a reaper," Agnes said in a low voice.

"What's that?"

Agnes gave me an annoyed look. "Don't you know anything?"

"In my defense, no, not when it comes to magic business."

"Reapers are sort of like these winged skeletons from the Under Dark dimension. They're incredibly fast and they are terrifying judgement assassins."

"A what now?"

"They kill things for breaking rules."

"And you decided to put one of these things in charge of the forbidden section of the library?"

"I know it seems like a bad idea, but Reapers actually make brilliant guardians, they have absolutely zero desire for power. Above all else they have a huge hard on for making sure everyone follows the rules, so they're ideal candidates for librarians."

I had to admit that one made me chuckle. "But these things assassinate people?"

"Not people. Hela worked as an assassin in the Under Dark, so she was responsible for offing demons that ventured to earth and unfairly took control of humans. Like I said, she looks and sounds very scary, but she's very strict about the rules, and she cares a lot about the books under her care."

"Couldn't she have done something about Big Tony and his boys then?"

"Nah, as far as Hela is concerned her duties end outside the forbidden section."

"And the mist and the gloom?" I said, looking around at this strange nightmare scape we found ourselves in.

"Apparently this is what it's like back in the Under Dark. This is how Reapers like things. To us this might seem like a cold and unpleasant hell, but for Hela it's a sunny day in a flowery meadow. And hey, the entire time she's been in charge of the forbidden section we've never had a book go missing, so you know she's doing a good job. Even those imps couldn't get in here, Hela saw to that!"

A few more steps brought us to a bookshelf ahead of us. Agnes muttered an incantation under her breath and two lanterns appeared in her hands, igniting the misty gloom around us. She handed one to me. For the most part the mist just reflected the light back, so we couldn't see much more than a few feet away from our position, but we could make out the titles on the spines of the books in front of us at least.

I could feel thick bands of magic pulsing off the books, throbbing through the air like an invisible cord. It was like a bell was ringing, but there was no sound, just the feeling of something moving through me.

Motes of purple light moved slowly through the air, and as we got closer to the books, I could hear a faint crackling sound. My fingertips prickled with the presence of strong magical energy.

"These five shelves contain every book we have on the mirror dimension," Agnes said, waving her lantern over the selection.

"Where do we start?" I asked, feeling bewildered by the choice.

"Your guess is as good as mine. I'd stay away from the tall black books on the top shelves, those are gnostic scrolls written by a group of insane warlocks. Those guys loved to play around with dangerous magic, the mirror dimension being no exception."

"Sounds like the kind of thing that would have been right up mom's avenue," I pointed out.

"Trust me," she said. "Just stay away from those books. Anything on the other shelves is fair game. I'll start at this end; you start at that one. Let your intuition guide you, and double check with me if you're unsure about anything. We'll meet back in the middle."

"Uh... okay," I said, already feeling very unsure about this. Agnes wondered off into the mist, the darkness quickly swallowing all sign of her lamplight. Gulping down my nerves, I made my way over to the left side of the shelf and started at that end. Some of the books looked so old I wasn't sure I could even get them off the shelf. The first one that I did try to move, the spine came away from the book and crumbled into pieces.

"Not that one then..." I said to myself.

I wondered along the bookshelf, looking at the rather unappealing collection of books sitting in front of me. It was hard to describe, but just the thought of touching most of them felt quite nauseating, like my body was already rejecting whatever dark contents lay within their pages.

After a few minutes of aimless searching, I felt like I should have done something by now, so I picked up the book nearest to me and held it in my hand, my grip trembling slightly at the strong throngs of energy coming from the tome.

Surviving the Mirror Dimension by Freda Dumas.

"Let's see what you have to say then..." I said, opening up the old book. As I did so a gust of cold wind rushed out and swept right through me, making me shiver. I flicked to one of the first pages in the book and scanned its contents. The book appeared to be a journal written by a long-dead witch that seemed to be something of a thrill seeker.

Beyond her personal accounts of getting in and out successfully, I felt like the book wasn't much use, so I put it back and walked along a little more. It had been about ten minutes now since Agnes and I had split up, so I shouted her name into the mist, but no response came.

There was still no sign of her lamplight, but I'd been walking along this shelf for the past few minutes. How long could it be exactly?

"Agnes?!" I called again. Silence breathed back from the mist. "Okay," I muttered to myself. "I'm seriously starting to get creeped out now." I began walking more quickly, adamant that I should find my accomplice before doing any more book searching.

After a dozen quick paces, I realized something rather troubling, the bookshelf was no longer on my left, and I turned around frantically in every direction I noticed I could see nothing but the endless veil of blinding mist in every direction. "Agnes!" I shouted. "Agnes where are you!"

I began to walk back in the direction I thought the bookcase would be, but I found myself lost in the endless ocean of fog. *Okay Zora don't panic. This is the perfect cocktail for a panic attack, but don't have one now! It's just you and Agnes in here!*

And if there was anything in here, it would be able to find me straight away because of the lantern. *Oh crap.*

I don't know why I did it—I mean, I do know why, it was fear—but I turned the lantern off in the hopes that I'd be able to see something through the fog. As it happened, I could make out the distant shapes of the giant shadowy bookcases, but I saw something else as well, or should I say I heard something.

It came rapidly from the darkness, like the clicking of a large insect accompanied by the sound of many small branches breaking over and over. The dark figure swept past me in an instant, and as I turned to try and track it, it swept pass in another direction.

"Who's there?!" I shouted. "Show yourself!"

The huge shadow rushed past me several more times from different directions until it disappeared. Hands trembling, I relit the lantern Agnes gave me and readied my wand too. Something was out there in the mist, and it seemed like I was about to find out what.

"Agnes? This isn't funny!" I called.

"Agnes?" a voice came from behind me. "I'm not Agnes."

Hairs standing on the back of my neck, I turned around very slowly, the lamplight illuminating the tall and haunting figure before me. She had a normal woman's face, but there was no flesh or muscle on the rest of her body, it was just a skeleton. For the most part the proportions looked almost human, except for the lower parts of her legs, the bones arranged in a way that reminded me more of a fast land predator. She wore black hooded robes, the fabric tattered to shreds and floating around her slowly as though moving through invisible water. In one hand she held a tall black staff, gnarled and twisted, it looked like it was hewn from some sort of marble.

Fear rose through me instantly as I looked upon this strange creature. I swallowed my nerves and stumbled back. "Who, who are you?" I stammered.

"My name is Hela, I am the keeper of the forbidden section," she said. With a flash of movement, she circled around me and came back to her original position, moving so quickly I could hardly keep track of her. The features of her face were sharp, the hair atop of her head dark and glistening.

"What have you done with Agnes?" I asked, my wand still at the ready. I was quite sure I wouldn't be able to take on this creature, but I would try my best at the least.

"That is what I came to find out," she said, her voice a strange sort of whisper. It was like metal upon stone. In the distance there was a loud boom, Hela jerked her head to the right, her feline-like pupils reducing to razor thin slits. "We are not the only ones in here," she said with a deathly whisper. Can you fight, witch?"

"Not very well," I admitted.

"Then it's time you improved, quickly. The mist aids me, but for you it is an inhibitor. Once we get close, I will move the mist, then you make your attack. You have to fight without hesitation if you want to save Agnes."

"From what?" I said, barely able to keep up. "What is going on here?"

"By my count there are five intruders, not including yourself and the librarian. Witches, the lot of them, each of them wearing hooded robes."

"The Sisters of the Shade," I gasped. They must have followed me here to make another attack.

"Prepare your killing magic, for they have prepared theirs. I can feel it," Hela warned.

"Absolutely not," I said, quickly scanning through my head for all the effective combat spells I could think of. "We need them alive. Do not kill them."

Hela sneered at me, as though she found the idea highly offensive. "Suit yourself," she growled. "Follow me, stay close. When I give the word prepare to make your attack. I cannot harm humans, the best I can do is aiding you with distraction. Otherwise, you're in this alone."

I followed the reaper through the mist, my wand ready for whatever lay ahead of us. Hela walked in a crouched fashion; her skeletal body curled up like a spring waiting to explode. Even at this crouched height she was still a good foot taller than me. I couldn't imagine how tall she was at full standing height.

Despite her size she moved without making sound. After a minute of walking, she turned back and whispered to me. "They are just ahead. They have the librarian bound. We must attack quickly once the mists clear. Got it?"

"Got it," I said. "And no killing."

Still moving through the mist, I saw the faint silhouette of a group up ahead. They were standing in a circle, and it looked like each of them was facing out. The group was talking in low voices.

"Well, where is she?!"

"I don't know!"

"We have to find her, quick!"

Hela motioned for me to stop, and we crouched low. We were only about ten feet away from the group now. "I'll move around the other side and flank them. Once I whistle the mists will move. I'll distract them, then you start firing on them from behind. Got it?"

"I think so," I said. With that Hela disappeared into the mists. She circled around the group, and I found myself surprised that they didn't see her. After disappearing across to the other side I held my breath so I wouldn't miss the signal.

Hela's shrill whistle punctured through the silence and then the mists in front of me vanished, revealing the five hooded witches. Agnes was in the middle, bound and gagged. Beyond the group I saw movement as Hela straightened up to her full towering height and extended four sets of arms, her eyes were glowing with ferocious energy, like a soldier keen for battle. In that moment she was terrifying, and I was glad she was on our side.

"Look out! Look out!" members of the group began to react. One by one they turned on Hela and fired their wands, beams of deadly magic crackling through the air.

Hela threw her head back and cackled, darting around the beams like it was no problem at all. "Excuse me ladies, but I need to see your membership card!"

"Another, behind us!" one of the dark witches shouted. Two of them turned around and pointed their wands at me. The next thing I knew two beams of killing magic were soaring my way.

The fight was on.

CHAPTER 18

I jumped out of the way of the two deadly attacks and hit the ground with a roll. In an instant I was back on my feet again, my wand pointed at the two witches as I prepared my attack.

"*Forca Apasti!*" I roared. The recoil from the spell blasted me back on to the ground, left to watch helplessly for a moment as a condensed projectile of wind roared through the air and hit both of the witches trying to kill me. It caught them both on the shoulder and sent them spinning back into the mists, far beyond Hela.

Two down, three to go.

Looking back to the fight I saw the air thick with the crisscross of deadly magical beams. Hela weaved and flashed around them all the while, cackling as she distracted the witches. She may not have been able to attack, but she was definitely proving her use. With the three witches distracted I hurried over to Agnes, who was tied up and writhing on the ground. I dropped to my knees and used a burning incantation to remove the ties, rushing off into the mists so I could get her to safety.

We reached a bookcase and took shelter behind it while gathering our breaths. "Cowards jumped me while I was in the middle of researching books!" she hissed. "They broke my wand too!"

"It's okay, Hela and I have got this. Are you okay?" Even though I *knew* that Agnes was actually an eighty-year-old woman, her childlike appearance made me worry about her more.

"I'm fine, now go and kick their candy asses!" she hissed. As she said the words a strange golden glow came over her body and Agnes appeared slightly younger. "Son of a—!" she began to curse before stopping herself.

I ran back towards the battlefield and found that it was chillingly quiet. There was no sign of Hela or the three remaining witches. As I ran into the cleared area, I skidded to a halt immediately and readied my wand.

"There!" a voice shouted to my right. Before I could react one of the dark witches sprung out of the mists and hurled something at me with her wand. Whatever it was, it hit me like a bowling ball, I flung back through the air and hit the ground ten feet behind me, my body tumbling across the ground until I came to a stop, winded and gasping. "Over here!" I heard my attacker shout.

I pushed myself up onto all fours, still gasping for air. Without the ability to speak my ability to defend myself had drastically been reduced. Mustering up what strength I had, I held my wand like it was a knife and dragged the tip across the ground as I drew a faint magic symbol. Once it was done, I rolled away from the symbol a few more feet and saw my attacker come through the mist.

"There you are," she said, a dark smile spreading over her young face. This witch couldn't be more than twenty years old, but somehow, she had chosen this dark path. "I'm sorry to do this, I would have preferred taking you alive, but the master says you have to die."

The young witch raised her wand, and the tip began to glow bright red. She took a step forward onto the symbol I had etched across the floor and screamed as the spell launched her into the air and out of sight.

The symbol was something I'd learned in Amos' magical classes, an enchanted glyph that acted like a high-powered catapult once something stepped onto it. I had no intention of launching my attacker quite that high and I cringed to think what would happen when she hit the ground again.

"Nali? Nali? Where are you?!" a voice came from the mist, it seemed that another one of my attackers was coming this way. I pushed myself to my feet and started hobbling off in the opposite direction, praying I could get some time before I had to fight again.

Fate wasn't on my side however, as I ran through the mists, I went headfirst into one of the dark witches, we both bounced off one another, me keeping my footing and her hitting the floor. She was a tiny mousy-blonde woman, with an expression of fear on her face.

"Don't kill me, don't kill me!" she gasped, throwing her wand to the ground. "I surrender!"

I pointed my wand at her and shouted a binding spell. Thick lengths of cord shot out and wrapped around her body, making sure she'd do no more harm. With one final witch to go I hobbled into the mists, moving back to the clearing where Hela and I had begun our attack. As I came into the clearing, I saw the final witch was already waiting for me there, her wand clasped in her hand.

"You're even trickier than I anticipated," she said. "Bravo."

"It's over. You're the last one, and you're outnumbered. Let's end this now. Surrender."

"No, I don't think I will. From where I'm standing, you're the one that's outnumbered. Your skeleton friend is preoccupied elsewhere, and now I have you all alone. How about we make things fair. You take the first shot."

"We don't have to do this," I said.

The dark witch shrugged. "I do."

"Fine. Suit yourself." I threw my wand up and sent a projectile hurtling at the witch, enough to knock her down and wind her. To my surprise the projectile passed straight through her. She stood there and laughed it off. "Okay. Now it's my turn."

The witch clapped her hands together and all of a sudden twelve identical copies of her were standing in formation in front of me. They spread out quickly until they had me surrounded in a circle.

"So," they all said in unison, their voices echoing all around. "Still think you have us outnumbered?"

Without any further warning the twelve identical copies lifted their wands and sent out bolts of killing magic. I threw my hands around me and summoned another orb of golden light, the first few spells bouncing off the shield harmlessly. It was the same trick I'd used with the imps, but this time I could feel that the attacking magic was more intense. The shield hummed with each hit and the light was starting to crack.

I began firing back, turning and attacking each clone surrounding me, desperate to try and find the real one. To my dismay none of my attacks landed. It seemed that all of the witches were projections.

As one they all threw their heads back and cackled. "See the power you can have? Join the Shade, and the master will bestow a gift upon you. He gave me the power to copy myself. You can't defeat my images, only the real me."

I crouched low as a bolt of deadly magic blasted a hole clean through my defensive shield. It wouldn't be long until the clones destroyed the orb completely, and then I would be utterly defenseless.

Think Zora, think!

Another hole blasted through the shield, this projectile narrowly missing my face by inches. The witches closed in, tightening their circle and laughing all the while.

Just then I saw more lights flashing through the mist. I turned and saw Hela on the circle's edge, surrounded by another group of the witch's false images. Each one was blasting her with rays of light. "Wick!" she shouted. "I cannot see for the light! The real witch must be close by! Use something big!"

Big? Big? What spell did I know that was big? The only thing that came to mind straight away was a fire spell that Amos had hinted at a couple of weeks ago, but we hadn't actually covered it yet.

I envisioned a large ball of fire erupting from my position and spreading out through the surrounding area. If the real witch was nearby the chances were good that I could hit her. It would take a lot of magic though, I had to give it everything I got to improve my chances of reaching her.

I had no idea what the incantation was, so I just gripped my wand tightly, closed my eyes and tried to imagine the end result. As I did so my wand started to shake violently, and I felt a huge surge of explosive power erupt from the ground beneath me. I opened my eyes and saw a vast ball of fire erupt across the circle and out into the mists, vaporizing the fake witch copies and illuminating the dark chamber.

My energy completely spent, I collapsed to the floor, my chest rising and falling rapidly after the fight. It couldn't have been more than five minutes from start to finish, but the adrenaline left me feeling wiped. The dark chamber was suddenly silent again, but I heard someone screaming out in pain in the mists.

"Put it out, put it out!" the voice wailed.

I pushed myself to my feet and saw fire just ahead of me through the fog. I walked forward and found the last witch, rolling around on the ground frantically and batting at her robes, trying to douse the fire from my last attack. With a last breath I used magic to bind her and blew out the fire.

"You'll regret this!" she hissed. "The master won't be happy!"

"Oh, shut up," Agnes said as she emerged from the mists. She picked up the witch's wand and gagged her. Just then Hela came out of the shadows, casting a derisory look at the captured witch.

"That's all of them," she said in her whisper like voice. "This one is very cunning, very clever. Distracted me with her copies and left me blind."

"Where are the others?" I asked. "We should round them up."

We spent the next five minutes finding and binding the remaining witches. The two I blasted at the start of the fight were twenty feet back from where they'd started, both unconscious. Obviously the other two were already bound, there was the meek witch that had fallen over, and the witch that could make copies of herself. It just left the witch that I had launched into the air with my enchanted glyph.

"I'm worried the last one might be dead," I said regretfully.

"Zora!" Agnes said in surprise. Hela however looked delighted.

"That's it. Tell me what you did," she grinned.

"It was an accident. I launched her into the air, but way too high. There's no way she could have survived that fall coming back down."

We scanned the area for a body but couldn't find anything. "What's to say she came down?" Hela asked. "Wait right here."

The tall reaper disappeared in a flash, leaving me and Agnes to watch over the captured witches. The only one currently making a fuss was the copy witch, but she wasn't too much nuisance thanks to Agnes' gag.

A few minutes later Hela returned with the other witch slung over her shoulder. She dropped her onto the ground—not gently might I add—and I fired a binding spell.

"How on earth is she alive?" I asked, grateful that magic hadn't made me a murderer just yet.

"I found her clinging to the rafters for dear life," Hela said, nodding her head to the high ceilings above us. There was an extensive network of shadowy beams crisscrossing the roof. "She about passed out when she saw me, scared the life out of her."

"That's all the witches accounted for then," I said.

"Now we just need to figure out how they got in here," Agnes murmured. She went over to the copy witch, who appeared to be the group leader, and ripped out her gag. "Spill the beans, how did you get in here?" Agnes spat.

The copy witch just laughed in her face. She turned away from Agnes and looked at me. "You think this is over? It's just beginning. The master will send more. Before long you'll be overrun. There's no running!" she cackled.

"I didn't run this time, I stood my ground and fought."

"And she kicked your lily butts," Agnes added.

The copy witch sneered. "You're going to get what's coming. We'll make sure of that."

"The only thing that's coming to you is the inside of a jail cell," Agnes said. "That reminds me, I should call the MCI and get them to clear up this mess."

Not long after that a man and a woman appeared in a puff of

nauseating pink smoke. They were both dressed like old-time detectives and had a sausage dog with them. It was clear from their garish suits—green and pink pinstripes—and their elaborate entrance that they were all magical.

"Henry and Barbara Pendragon," the woman said in a posh English accent, coming up and shaking my hand.

"And this is Horatio," the man added, gesturing to the sausage dog besides them.

"Bloody hell, what do we have here?" the sausage dog said in a voice even posher than his owners. "Five witches all subdued by one? Marvelous work." He looked up at me. "Ever considered joining Magic Crimes Investigation?"

"I had help," I said, nodding to Hela and Agnes. "And I'm not interested, but thanks."

One by one the trio of magical agents went around the group and put them in proper magical restraints. The man and the sausage dog escorted them out through a pink-rimmed portal, while the woman, Barbara Pendragon, remained behind to talk momentarily.

"So, you're the prismatic witch I've heard so much about," she said with a smile.

"It seems everyone has heard about me," I remarked with surprise.

"Yes, news of a prismatic witch will undoubtedly spread fast. It seems the Sister of the Shades are growing bolder. You did well to hold your own against five of them."

"To be honest I couldn't have done it without Hela or Agnes. They both helped too."

Barbara nodded, though I could tell that she thought I was being too humble. "Nevertheless, I'm very impressed Zora Wick. Even for a beginner your skills are quite advanced. We've run IDs on the five witches, four of them are juniors, and the witch that can copy herself was their leader. It's normal for Shade witches to travel in small groups like this."

Just then the small sausage dog hopped back through the pink-rimmed portal and trotted over to us, sniffing along the ground as he went.

"How did they get in here though?" I asked Barbara.

"That's what I'm here to find out," Horatio said. He stopped and looked over at Hela, who was watching over the proceedings silently. "You're the one that watches over this place, right?"

"That's right," she said, her ghostly voice sounding like glass on rock.

"Any idea how five dark witches can get into a secure facility like this?" Horatio asked.

"My guess would be one of the books. There are lots of books in here containing serious dark magic."

Horatio lifted his nose to the air and started sniffing again.

"Have you got the dark witches' scent, Horatio?" Barbara asked.

"Yes, yes," he said quickly. "It smells like they came in over here. Follow me!"

CHAPTER 19

We were a strange looking group to say the least. There was Horatio, the small talking sausage dog at the front, me, Agnes—who looked five but was obviously much older—Barbara Pendragon in her pink and green pinstriped suit, and then the reaper Hela following at the back of the group.

Horatio trotted quickly through the mists, and Agnes produced two more lanterns to help illuminate the darkness. After a few minutes of following the scent and jogging down dark aisles of books, Horatio stopped at a shelf where there was an open book on the ground.

"This is it!" he said cheerily. "The trail stops here! This is where they came in!"

"Everybody stand back and let me take a look," Barbara said.

We all made space and Barbara crouched down to get a closer look at the book. As she put her hands upon its pages a black vortex opened, and wind started to rush about everywhere. Barbara quickly closed the book and picked it up. "This is it alright. It's a portalis."

"What now?" I asked.

"A portalis. Two books that can be linked together to make a magic portal with one another. The question is, what's it doing here?" Barbara directed the question at Agnes and Hela.

Agnes shrugged her shoulders. "Don't look at me. We have a lot of questionable books in here, but none of them should let things through without permission. I've curated all the books in here personally."

Hela nodded in agreement. "This book is unfamiliar to me."

"Can you check the book?" Barbara asked. "See if it's in the library catalogue?"

Agnes snapped her fingers and a large green book appeared in front of her, hovering in the air. With a quill in one hand and another flicking through pages, she searched through the tome until she happened upon the thing she was looking for. "Nope, this book is not a part of the library catalogue. Someone must have slipped it in here!"

"Impossible!" Hela said with aghast. "They would have to have slipped past me!"

"Unless they were meant to be here," I pointed out. Everyone looked at me.

"What are you suggesting, Wick?" Barbara Pendragon asked.

"This is the forbidden section, but it doesn't mean that no one can come in here. You have a list of people that have access to the forbidden section, right? What if one of them snuck in here and left the book, knowing that I'd come back at some point."

"We need to see the list of people that have access to the forbidden section," Barbara said to Agnes. "Chances are one of the people on that list is colluding with the Sisters of the Shade."

"Sure thing," Agnes fumbled. "Just give me a moment to find it." Agnes stepped to the side and started looking through her large floating book again. Barbara and Horatio started talking quietly amongst themselves and Hela came over to me.

"Why were you in here, out of interest?" she asked. "Perhaps I can be of assistance."

"I'm looking for books on the mirror dimension. I think my mom might be trapped there."

"What's her name? I will check my own records," Hela said.

"Tabitha. Tabitha Wick."

Hela gave a firm nod and then turned around to leave. "I will be back shortly. Don't leave." With that the tall skeleton woman disappeared into the mists.

"Here we are," Agnes said, having found her list. She turned the book around so we could see the current wizards and witches in Compass Cove that had access to the restricted section of the library. "There are fourteen names in total!"

DERONI KRAUSS. *Torin Tenebris. Arabella Wax. Maddox Everbleed. Amos Aposhine. Isabel Knotley. Delilah Conners. Zambo Talbot. Tabitha Wick. Evelyn Barclay. Tempest Grimsbane. Solomon Hunt. Misty Norwood. Zora Wick.*

"ARE ALL THESE PEOPLE STILL ALIVE?" I asked, peering over the list. I actually recognized three names, my mother's, mine, and my magical teacher, Amos.

"Crikey, now you're asking," Agnes said in a flustered manner. "I don't exactly do regular checkups on my library members."

"Can you tell us when each member last came in?" Barbara suggested.

"I have a log for member visitors, I'll check that." Agnes snapped her fingers and held her hand out expectantly. Nothing happened, so she snapped her fingers again and then a tattered book spine, half-covered in something resembling saliva, landed in her palm. Agnes shrieked and let the slimy object hit the floor. "Those damn imps must have got to it!"

"Great, so we have no way of seeing who has been in here?" Horatio asked in a deflated manner. "Another lead gone!"

"We have backup records," Agnes said quickly. "Jake transcribes all the records at the end of the month. He did it just before those imps came in and took over. I'll have to ask him about it, but word to the wise, he's not exactly the quickest." Jake was Agnes' second in command, the large jackal-headed guardian that helped to overlook the library.

"Have him do that," Barbara said. "Once we find out who's been in here most recently, we can narrow down our suspect list. Until then we should get going, eh, Horatio? There's plenty to keep us busy back at MCI headquarters." She turned and looked at me, handing me a card. "Here's my card, Wick. Get in touch if you need anything. Agnes, we'll be confiscating the portalis book, you understand?"

"Get it out of here! I don't want that thing!"

Horatio and Barbara disappeared through a pink-rimmed portal, leaving me and Agnes by ourselves. "Well," she said. "Talk about an eventful first visit to the forbidden section. I'm sorry things got so messed up, Wick."

"On the contrary I should probably be the one apologizing. I'm the one they were looking for."

"Nonsense, Wick. We're all in this together. I need to keep a better eye on things around here. We'll have to do a deep scan and make sure this traitor didn't leave any more books behind!"

A figure came rolling quickly through the mists and I knew now that it was Hela. She stopped in front of us, with a book clutched in her hand. Its outer cover was covered in mirrored tiles only, no title or indication of an author. "This is the book your mother checked out the most," Hela rasped. She handed it to me. The book was surprisingly heavy.

"This has to hold some important information, right?" I asked Agnes. The head librarian yawned and shrugged her shoulders.

"Like I said, your guess is as good as mine. Put it on the ground and open it up, Wick. We'll see what the book has to say."

I set the book down on the ground and unclasped the latch holding the cover shut. I opened the book and didn't expect to find anything of consequence, but as soon as the pages parted something crazy happened.

"Ahhhh!" came a voice.

A pair of heeled feet shot out of the book and knocked me back onto the ground. A woman shot up into the air foot first, screaming all the while. The momentum carried her up in a slight arc until her feet came down and she crashed on top of me with another loud shriek.

She pushed herself up quickly, her wild brown hair a mess of tangles and knots. There was a manic look in her eyes, and she scrambled to her feet and looked around as though something was about to attack her.

After realizing the coast was clear she made an attempt to quickly straighten out her hair and dress. She held her hand out and helped me up from the ground. At once I realized who she was, but my tongue caught in my throat, my heart stopped in my chest.

"Flipping heck," she said and smiled, blowing a hair off her face. "I was starting to think I'd never get out of there!"

"M-Mom?!" I stammered, not quite believing what I was seeing.

"That's right, it's me sweetie!" she said, throwing her arms around me and giving me a crushing hug. "It's so good to finally do that."

Mom pushed herself back, still keeping her hands on my shoulders. "Agnes, you've gotten younger. Still cursing?"

"Unfortunately, yes."

"Hela," Mom said to the tall reaper woman. "Still as terrifying as ever."

"I try my best," Hela rasped back.

"Mom, where have you been? It's been twenty years. You look... you look so—"

"Young?" Yes, it's a consequence of being stuck in that dratted mirror dimension for over two decades darling. I suppose all clouds have a silver lining. Still, we haven't got much time. The cat is out of the bag now, and we've got work to do."

"But why did you—where did you—why—" I fumbled, trying to give order to the *many* questions rattling around my brain.

"Darling, I can appreciate you probably have a million and one questions, and I will answer them all in time, but first of all we need to summon a family meeting, at once. We're all in *very* grave danger. It's your father."

"Dad?"

"Your... real father, Zora. You may not know this, but the man that raised you isn't your real dad."

"Actually, I do know that. He caught me up to speed just the other night."

"Perfect, well that's one less thing to get out of the way," she said in a cheery manner.

"But who is my real father?" I asked.

"He's the damned psychopath in charge of the Sisters of the Shade," she said. "And he's coming here to kill us. Now, round up the troops. We need a family meeting."

* * *

I HAD ENTERED the library looking for my mother, and left having found her. As we stepped back out into the open world of Compass Cove, I saw her stop and take a moment to appreciate the world she had been missing from for all these years. Dark clouds were roiling overhead, and rain was starting to fall.

We made our way back to the bakery, which had already closed up for the day. Once inside, I locked the doors and headed upstairs with mom.

"This place is a lot nicer on this side of the mirror," she observed upon walking into the main apartment upstairs. "I only ever got a limited view on the other side."

Hermes, who was sitting on the kitchen counter and grooming himself, stopped what he was doing, and his mouth dropped open. "Zora, I think there must be something in that fancy cat food, because I'm seeing things. Your mother is here."

"You're not seeing things, Hermes, it's really her. She bounced out of a book in the restricted section of the library. She's been... trapped in the mirror dimension all these years?" I asked, pointing the last part of that statement to her. We hadn't actually had a chance to clear up what had happened yet.

"That's right. All will be explained in time. Good to see you

Hermes, you've haven't aged a day, in fact I'd say you've only gotten more handsome with time."

"I did miss you, Tabitha," Hermes said with a grin. "Ever the charmer. I take it you want something though, as you're laying it on so thick?"

She nodded her head. "As perceptive as you are glossy. Summon the family. We need a meeting."

"I'm on it!" he said, bolting off the counter and out of the room.

I found myself staring in bewilderment. "How on earth did you do that? He's never that cooperative around me!"

"Hermes? He's easy. Just butter him up and he's jelly in your hand." Mom walked into the apartment, taking in the surroundings. "I like what you've done with the place."

"To be honest I've not really done much at all. Most of this is Constance's."

"Such a shame what happened to her," Mom said with a shake of her head. She leaned to get a look at the sleeping time owl then pivoted away on her heels, wondering over to the large glass windows that overlooked the street below. Fat droplets of rain were coming down hard on the panes now. "It's good to be back," she said wistfully.

Not long after that the troops, and by that I mean my family, started to arrive, each one equally shocked to see the return of my mother. Sabrina and Celeste were the first ones to arrive, and mom met them with awkward hugs. To them she was the eccentric aunt that disappeared before either of them was born.

"I don't understand," Sabrina said. "Where have you been?"

"I'll explain when everyone is here darling," Mom said. "Sit down, I'll make some tea and cookies. Zora, can I borrow your wand?"

"You might not be able to use it," I pointed out. "I'm a prismatic witch." While most witches and wizards could switch wands, only I could use mine, with the exception of a few people.

"Yes, yes, I know. Pass it here."

I passed the wand over to mom and to my surprise I saw it light up with colors as she took it. Sabrina and Celeste looked equally surprised. "You can use it?" I gasped, watching as mom magicked up some tea and cookies.

"Yes darling, I'm prismatic too. Kept it a secret basically my whole life, Constance was the only other person that knew. Ah, speak of the devil!"

It was just then that Constance floated into the room, it looked like she had raced to get here. She stopped dead in her tracks and stared at my mother before breaking out in a wide grin. "I knew you were still alive," she said.

"I wish I could say the same about you sis," Mom said, opening her arms as Constance floated in for a ghostly hug. "How's the afterlife?"

"It's going great. I've just started a new women's acapella group. We're the talk of the town! Where have you been?"

"Sit down, I'll get to that once Zelda and mother arrive."

The next person to enter the room was Liza, our mysterious grandmother who very rarely made appearances. She was a stately woman and quite detached emotionally. I didn't get the impression that she disliked us at all, rather that she was just an extremely introverted person. We all grew quiet as she came into the room. Liza stopped and stared at my mom for a few moments, her eyes taking in the daughter that had been missing for over two decades.

Without a word she crossed the room, threw her arms around mom and held her like that for a long time. When she pulled away, I saw tears in her eyes. She wiped them away quickly and that cold composure came back over her.

"And where have you been?" she said in a clipped manner. "You had me scared to death. You don't look a year older!"

"Sit down mom, I'll explain when—"

Zelda came through the door then, dumping bags and backpacks onto the ground. I had no idea why she always carried so much crap around with her. She too took one look at mom and ran across the room to hug her. Zelda, who was arguably the most emotional one of the group, broke out bawling and it took several minutes to calm her down.

A SCONE TO PICK

"You're back! You're really back!" she wailed after several bouts of consolation. "I can't believe it!"

"Yes darling, mother's back. To be honest I never meant to leave for this long. I'm annoyed with myself for messing things up, I missed so much—" She paused and looked at both me and Zelda. "Still, if I'd stayed around things would have been much different, dare I say worse."

"Okay Tabitha," Grandmother Liza said, "Spill the beans. What's going on here? Where have you been? Why call a family meeting?"

"I take it everyone in here is familiar with the name Richard Desmond?" she said to the group. As she looked around the room everyone gave a nod of acknowledgment. Sabrina raised her hand. "No need to raise hands, Sabrina," Mom said. "It's a family meeting, not school. Speak freely."

"Zora won't know," she said. "She's still new to this magic business."

"I do know!" I countered. "Amos told me about him in my magic lessons." I looked at mom for clarification. "Richard Desmond was an evil wizard, right? He tried to take over the world in the 1990s, but then he just... disappeared?"

"Exactly! Or that's what the history books say at the very least. Anyway, he's the reason we've called this family meeting. He *did* disappear, but he's not gone. He's been resting, rebuilding his strength. After all he nearly died."

"How do you know all this?" Zelda asked.

"Because I'm the one that tried to kill him."

A stony silence filled room. Hermes decided to break it. "You always were a boss babe, Tabitha."

"Thank you, Hermes," mom replied.

"Tabitha, am I hearing this correctly? You tried to kill the evilest wizard of the last millennium?" Grandmother Liza asked. "How in heaven did you get close enough to him?"

"Because there was a time when we very close to one another," she admitted.

"How close are we talking here?" Zelda asked in amazement.

"Uh..." Mom began.

"I know that sound," Constance cackled. "They did the horizontal no-pants dance!"

"I think we're all old enough call it sex, Constance," Mom said sardonically.

"You had sex with that monster?!" Grandmother Liza roared, jumping up to her feet.

"Can everyone in the room over thirty please stop using the word sex?" Celeste asked timidly, holding her head in her hands.

"Yeah, let's get more with the times. They were *banging*," Hermes added. Sabrina spat out her drink.

Liza, still standing, looked at her daughter in horror. "Well, Tabitha, is it true? Did you sleep with that man? That man that killed hundreds of innocent humans?!"

Mom put her hands in the air, trying to steady the waters. "We had a relationship, but when we started dating, he was still a good man. There was a time when he was a good wizard, a great wizard even—but the change... it came on so fast. By the time it started, it was already too late. I was too involved. I couldn't get out."

At this point everyone in the room was looking at mom with some sort of confusion on their faces. "Why do I feel like you're leaving something out here?" Constance asked.

"Yes Tabitha, get to the point already," Grandmother Liza clipped. "It's been twenty years. We're all dying to hear why you decided to vanish."

Mom took a very deep breath and looked at everyone in turn, finally settling on me. "Zora, Richard Desmond is your father, and he's coming here for you."

"What?" I stammered.

"What?!" just about everyone else in the room said.

"That monster is my father?" I faltered.

A regretful nod preceded her answer. "Yes, and he needs you. When you were conceived it took a significant part of his power away. It's part of the reason I was able to defeat him. He has rested all these years, and he's gained some of that strength back. The only way to return to his former glory is to either recruit you or kill you. That is why the Sisters of the Shade want you so badly."

"Sorry, just to clarify," Hermes said, clearing his throat. "You're saying that Zora's real father is Richard Desmond, one of the most dangerous magicians of all time?"

"Yes," Mom answered. "And I went away to keep you safe. It's a long story."

"Better start talking then, before I miss Idol!" Constance barked.

"I think we're going to need more tea," Grandmother Liza said.

"And cookies," Celeste added. "A lot more cookies."

CHAPTER 20

Mom had the floor, and everyone looked at her with expectation. "There used to be a time when I couldn't talk about this, but those days are long gone now—I've been gone for so long that everyone assumes I'm dead anyway."

"You were always like this," Constance said. "Sneaking around. Vanishing without explanation. You were gone more than you were here. Ever since you turned sixteen it was like that."

"Sit down Constance... or should I say float down?" Mom looked genuinely unsure. "The reason for the secrecy is because I was sworn to it. When I was young a group approached me, a secret organization that wanted to recruit me for my abilities." Mom looked over at Grandmother Liza. "Constance is the only one that ever knew this, but I'm a prismatic witch."

"I know," Liza said dryly.

"You do?" Mom asked, looking surprised.

"Yes, but I respected your wishes to keep it secret. I can't say I don't blame you. It's a lot of fame, a lot of attention, but I'm your mother of course—you can't keep secrets from me. I know more about you than you think."

Not about the part where my father was a deranged killer, apparently.

"I kept my powers secret and pretended I was a run of the mill kitchen witch. I didn't want to stand out or be different, I wanted to be like everyone else. But... other people did end up noticing. Luckily for me they were good people."

"Those were the ones that recruited you?" Zelda asked. Mom nodded. "Who were they?"

"They are a secret magical organization, they call themselves—"

"MAGE?" I guessed.

Mom's eyes opened wide with shock. "How did you know?!"

"Let's just say it sounds familiar."

"Zora's boyfriend is in MAGE," Hermes explained. "He's the coolest. He's always fighting monsters and doing dope stuff."

Mom chuckled to herself. "So, MAGE are still going strong, eh? Good to hear it. Well, they're the ones that approached me, and I started working for them from a young age. I started out in a division that specializes in rooting out dark magic. I was good at the work, and I rose through the ranks quickly.

"It was at MAGE I met Richard for the first time. We hated each other at first. He was basically aristocracy at that point, very high up in the organization, another young starter like me who had progressed quickly. Not long after that he became the Sorcerer Supreme." Mom paused and looked at me. "That's akin to being president for magical folk, darling."

"Got it, thanks."

"Due to work circumstances Richard and I were pushed together. He was the one in charge, I was merely tasked with handling his security. I was his personal bodyguard, no one else could beat me in a magical duel. Richard and I practiced frequently and even he very rarely beat me."

"So, you regularly beat the crap out of Richard Desmond?" Sabrina asked, looking pretty enamored. "That's pretty cool."

Mom smiled. "At this point we were pretty much friends, and before long... we became more. Keep in mind he was still a good man at this point. The magic world looked up to and respected Richard with great admiration. Even I did. He was extremely charismatic and exceptionally sharp, he brightened even the darkest rooms. We kept our relationship secret, the position required that Richard kept no family or relationships, but we had several good years together."

For a moment mom trailed off, sitting in a contemplative silence, her eyes glazed over as she looked into her past.

"So, what went wrong?" Liza asked from the back of the room, her voice cutting through the silence. We all looked to Grandmother Liza, and then back to mom.

"There was a tactical operation, an important one. The Sisters of the Shade were more of a problem back then. Frequently abducting humans, turning witches and wizards to the dark side. We received intel providing the information of their suppose patron—"

"Patron?" I asked.

"The Sisters of the Shade receive their power from an unknown source, a demon that gives them power in return for their souls. For the exchange to work that demon has to have a secret abode somewhere here on the planet. We spent many years looking for it. To destroy it would destroy the dark cult once and for all. Then one day, we received a tip off. We followed it and sure enough it led us to the hidden temple harboring the patron."

"What happened then?" Celeste asked, sitting so far forward on her chair I thought she might fall off.

"It wasn't pretty. We took a great number of men and women with us, and over half died fighting to get inside. In the end we won, and the witches guarding the temple surrendered. The leader of the cult at the time was a witch named Beatrix Hollow. Richard told her to lay down her wand and that it was all over, but she fought… to the death. There was a black amulet around her neck, the magic item connecting her with the patron granting power to the cult."

"Why do I get the feeling I know what happened next…" Hermes said.

"I told Richard to destroy it, but all of a sudden it was like the thing had a hold on him. A change came over him, his eyes darkened. 'But

Tabitha, my darling, imagine the great things we could do with the power. We could change the world... we could rule it!'

"I knew then that I had to destroy the amulet, but when I tried to do so Richard deflected the spell, placed the amulet upon himself and used his newfound power to blast me back. He defeated me easily, I could no longer beat him. He told me to join him and serve at his side. I told him I couldn't do that."

"What did you do next?" Zelda asked.

"I... I ran. Richard tried to stop me, he tried to get the others to stop me too, but somehow, I managed to get out of there. At that point I was on the run, and over the next six months your father transitioned from a great man to the terrible tyrant. It all happened so fast, and all the while things were changing for me too. I'd fallen pregnant with you Zora, right before the change came over Richard."

"It happened before he became evil then?" I asked.

She nodded. "That's right. I didn't know it at the time, but as you grew inside me Richard was growing weaker. His tyranny continued because he had the power of the dark amulet, but he realized his strength was fading. Richard used his power to find me, he came to me in a dream. He asked for a meeting, just the two of us. He told me he regretted succumbing to the dark amulet and that he wanted my help to break free."

"Textbook trap," Hermes scoffed. "Don't tell me you fell for that one."

"Of course not," Mom said casually. "It was very obvious that Richard intended to imprison me at the least or kill me at the worst. I didn't get as far as I did by being so naïve. I did however decide to meet him."

"What?!" Sabrina gasped. "Why?!"

"Because I knew that it might be my last attempt to try and stop him. Although it had only been half a year Richard's reach had grown terrifically so. Most of the wizarding world was already under his grasp, and he had begun his assaults on humankind too. He had started rounding humans up and slaughtering them in their hundreds, he said it was a cleansing, that the new world would be a place only for those with magic!"

"Why have I never heard anything about this?" I asked. "In human history books?"

"After Richard Desmond disappeared his cult dismantled," Liza explained. "The wizarding world came together to clean up the mess he left behind. It took many years to erase the marks of his dark scourge." She looked back at Mom. "So, what happened at the meeting?"

Mom took a deep breath. "I knew that the only way I could meet with him and have an advantage if I appeared to be sympathetic to his cause. I pretended that I'd seen the error of my ways and come around to Richard's way of thinking. I agreed to the meeting, under the pretense that I would go there to fully submerse myself into his cult."

"So you went to the meeting under false pretenses," Celeste said. "But you planned to undermine him? That's badass."

"Exactly," Mom said. "We met at a remote location, and to my surprise it was just the two of us. I anticipated he might not uphold his end of the bargain, but he agreed. The power of the dark amulet had gone to his head, his ego was large, and with good reason too, he had never been more powerful. Zora was growing inside me though, and as she grew bigger, his natural power grew weaker." Mom paused for a moment to collect her thoughts.

"Well, what happened?" Liza asked. "Tell us!"

"Why don't I just show you?" Mom said. "With that she pointed the tip of my wand against the front of her head, and all of a sudden, the room grew dark until a new scene replaced it.

"What is this?" Sabrina gasped, watching as the scenery changed around us.

"Memory projection," Liza said with realization. "Extremely advanced magic. Tabitha, I must admit you still find ways to surprise me."

Mom nodded at something behind us, and we all turned to watch the scene play out. We were now standing in some sort of abandoned warehouse, watching from the sidelines as two lone figures walked in and stopped far apart from one another: my mother and father.

"When I entered the room, I didn't recognize the man before me. His eyes no longer held the same spark, his skin was so pale. He was supposed to be the strongest wizard on the planet, but I'd never seen him weaker," Mom said to us. Then the memory version of her and Richard started talking.

"I thought it was the power of the dark amulet draining me," he said to her, his voice echoing across the large room. "But the one that gives me power has told me different. They tell me you are with child. My child. I'm not supposed to have a child and hold this power as well. It's holding me back, Tabitha."

The image of my mother clenched her fists. "Then it seems you need to make a choice. The dark path ahead of you, or the child. There's still time to go back Richard. We can undo all this."

The dark eyed man scoffed. "What? And spend the rest of my life rotting in solitary confinement? I don't think so Tabitha. The cleansing has already begun. Once I have my full power back this world will belong to us once and for all. The only person that has to make a choice is you, and from our previous conversation I assumed you'd already made it. You came here to join me, didn't you?"

"What do you intend to do with this child?" Mom asked him.

For a second, he said nothing back. His gaze flitted to the floor. "If I want to completely align myself with the dark amulet, the child will have to go Tabitha, I'm sorry, but there's no other way. Join me, surrender the child, and we can rule everything together." He held out his hand and smiled. "It's... it's really the only way."

Mom smiled, but then she lowered her head and let the warmth go. "I'm afraid that's not possible, you're not the man I fell in love with."

Richard's smile fell too. "Then... I'm afraid you'll have to die as well. I'm sorry to do this Tabitha, but the ends will justify the means."

The current day version of mom turned to those of us watching the memory. "It was then that I knew he was going to kill me. I anticipated this was going to happen, and as such I'd spent the last few weeks secretly preparing a spell, some of the strongest magic I'd ever attempted."

Without warning the dark-eyed man lifted his hand and let loose a bolt of red lightning. It went straight for mom, and she threw her hands up just in time to deflect it. Despite her efforts the spell still sent her flying back and tumbling across the ground. She lay still for a moment and then slowly pushed herself up, the dark-eyed man walking towards her.

"Such a shame," he said with a shake of his head. "We could have done so much together."

"You will never take my child," mom rasped, her nose bleeding as she looked up at him. He stood right over her now, one handheld against her head. He laughed.

"It's too late, I already have."

Just then a brilliant ball of white light exploded forth from my mother and sent the dark-eyed man hurling across the air, almost travelling the full length of the large, abandoned warehouse. Mother collected herself, stood up and ambled over to him, one of her arms clearly broken as she hobbled over.

He lay there on the ground, his body smoking and his skin charred, in a much worse condition than my mother. "Why?" he said, his voice a broken whisper.

"You know why," she responded with tears in her eyes. "I'm sorry Richard, but someone has to stop you." With that mom held out her hand and white magic started to brim on her fingertips. Before she could unleash the spell however the dark amulet started glowing on Richard's chest, and he disappeared in a flash of red light.

The memory broke away and we all returned to our apartment once more.

"And that's what happened," Mom said. "He disappeared before I could completely destroy the amulet. I think his patron teleported him away to safety, probably back to the Under Dark from which it came. I had little choice but to get out of there, it wouldn't be long before his supporters found out what happened and tracked me down.

"Richard was as good as dead. The spell I hit him with initially should have killed any normal person, but the amulet kept him alive. I knew then that I had to hide you Zora, so I took you to Nolan, the man that became your father. You were to grow up with a normal life and know nothing about magic, that way your father would never find you," Mom explained.

"But you didn't disappear," Zelda pointed out. "You came back here, to Compass Cove. You hung around long enough to have me!"

Mom nodded. "I helped clean up the mess that Richard left behind. Everyone did their part. No one quite knew where Richard had gone, but we all sensed his energy was somewhere else. The cult disbanded and things returned to normal. His followers were rounded up and imprisoned. Then for a while life even seemed ordinary again. I even met someone, and we ended up having you Zelda, but shortly after that I felt something, something uncomfortably familiar. Richard was back, I don't know how I knew, I just did. Not long after that he came to me in a dream again. He told me he would find Zora and kill her. He just needed to get the information out of me first."

"Took about a good male role model," Hermes said with another roll of his eyes.

"What did you do then?" Sabrina asked. Both she and Celeste were hanging onto every word. To be honest, we all had.

"I knew that as long as Richard could find me, he had a way of finding Zora, so I decided to hide. There was only one place his magic couldn't look."

"The mirror dimension," I said.

Mom nodded. "I knew the risks. It's a dangerous place, hard to traverse and even harder to keep your sanity. It's a fractal plane, where even the simplest hallway can look like a complex carpet pattern from the seventies... one that you're trapped inside.

Once again Mom gave us another brief glimpse of her memories, projecting some complicated geometric maze with countless corridors and levels. She dispelled the memory quickly, the apartment coming back into focus. Just that brief glimpse was unpleasant and disorientating.

"I think I'm going to be sick," Zelda said, holding a hand over her mouth.

"I messed up however," Mom said. "I didn't intend to stay there for so long. I planned to come back when you turned five Zora. I was that age when my magic started to kick in, and I hoped it would be the same for you. Unfortunately, I was trapped, and ended up staying much longer. If I was anyone else, I would have gone mad, but I had to stay sane, I knew that one day I would see my daughters again and have to fight for them."

"Plus, you were already crazy," Constance added, "You'd have to be to voluntarily put yourself in the mirror dimension."

"So, what do we do now?" Liza asked. "You say this brute is back again? Coming here for Zora?"

"That's right. I don't know when he'll make his attack, but he either wants you to join him or die, Zora. As far as he's concerned, they are the only choices. He's not as strong as he used to be, but I'm pretty sure he still has the dark amulet on his side, so he's still extremely dangerous."

"But what do we do?" I asked, reiterating Liza's question. "Do we know when or how he'll come?"

Mom shook her head. "No, but I can feel his presence, and I know that he is somewhere near to the town. If I had to bet on it, I'd say the attack will happen soon. The best thing we can do is pretend that we're all going on with our lives as normal but be prepared at a moment's notice if we need to fight."

"That's it?" I asked. "Just carry on with everyday life and wait for this attack to happen? Why not go out and find them? We can strike first. End this once and for all."

"We are stronger here in the town," Liza pointed out. "If we go to them, we're immediately on the backfoot. Richard Desmond is a cunning magician, and any base he has constructed will be full of traps and pitfalls. I think Tabitha is right on this one. Let them come to us, make them think that we don't suspect a thing."

"Then it's settled," Liza said, standing to her feet and picking up her things. "We all carry on acting like everything is normal. Tabitha, it's probably best if you stay out of sight until we apprehend Desmond. I will have the witch council on standby for instant response for any upcoming threats, but I won't give them any details."

And just like that we found ourselves all caught up with mom's mysterious past. Her disappearance, the reason that Zelda and I had grown up apart, and even the reason she'd been gone for so long.

There had been so many revelations over the past few days it was hard to keep them straight in my head, but the hardest thing of all was carrying on and pretending that everything was normal. After we all said our goodbyes, I showed mom to Constance's spare room. She was so tired that her eyes closed pretty much the moment her head hit the pillow. I walked into my room and also flopped onto the bed, letting out a long yawn.

"So, pretty crazy night, huh?" Hermes chirruped and jumped up beside me. I scratched his head lightly between the ears.

"How am I supposed to carry on acting like everything is normal knowing that my father and a group of dark withes are coming here to kill me?" I asked him.

"That's a tricky one," Hermes admitted. "Whenever I'm stressed about something I take a long nap."

"Not likely," I said, glancing at the time on the bedside clock. "I've got to be up in five hours to start the morning bake."

"Well, sugar might help—sugar always helps!"

I couldn't disagree with that one.

CHAPTER 21

"Okay girls, I think that's everything sorted for the day," I said to Rosie and Daphne as we wrapped up the morning bake. It had been a busy morning getting things sorted. I did fall asleep in the end, but to be honest I probably only had one or two hours sleep before it was time to get up and start baking.

Once the bakery opened and the morning rushed passed, I hung up my apron, changed into a pair of clean clothes (Wardrobe was being much more cooperative since her restoration with Chang) and I went out to meet Hudson for coffee.

"There's my girl," he said, greeting me with a kiss and a big squeeze. "How have you been?"

"It's been… an interesting couple of days, put it that way!" I said with a chuckle. Although Hudson and I hadn't seen one another we'd been keeping in touch via phone, and I'd kept him up to date through calls and messages.

"I'll say. Let's go inside and get a drink. You can give me the full details."

We found a quite table upstairs and for the next hour solid I unloaded everything onto Hudson. The ghost of my father visiting me in my bedroom, the fight with the dark witches in the library, finding my mother after two decades of her disappearing, and everything she had told us about the identity of my real dad.

"So yeah…" I said in summation after a very long time of talking. "Turns out my real dad is a crazy evil wizard, and he's actually the one in charge of the Sisters of the Shade. He's coming here to kill me or abduct me, and I have to act like everything is normal."

Hudson just sat there for a few long moments, blinking at me as he tried to process everything. "Pretty normal week then?" he jested.

I couldn't help laughing, Hudson always knew how to get me. "You might say that, yeah. Anyway. Enough about me. How has your week been? How are things with the giant lake monster? I trust everything went okay as the town wasn't squished to a pulp."

"I'm happy to report that the kraken is asleep and well. Turns out it was just a sensor malfunction. Still didn't change the fact had I had to dive down to the bottom of the lake and replace the darned thing."

"How big is this thing exactly?" I asked. "Like… bigger than a bus?"

Hudson laughed and then realized I was being serious. "Oh, yeah, it's bigger than a bus. Its tentacles might be the same diameter as a bus though."

The hairs instantly stood up on the back of my neck. "I think I'm going to be sick. Say, have you heard anything from Blake since he left? I've messaged him a few times but heard nothing in reply. I'm considering worrying as his creepy replacement said that werewolf politics usually end in fights to the death."

"That Niles guy yeah? Yeah, I crossed paths with him the other day actually. He wanted to introduce himself to me," Hudson said.

"What did you make of him?" I asked.

Hudson looked around the room while thinking. "I guess the word sociopath comes to mind. I'm not sure. He's pale, gaunt, his hair is all messy and he's kind of dead behind the eyes. Still, if Blake chose him as his replacement, he must be good."

"Really? Because you're assessment of him was like 90% negative," I pointed out.

He tilted his head to concede the point. "Maybe so, but like I said, I trust Blake's judgement. Don't you?"

"I do, but that Chang guy told me three people would try and betray me to the Sisters of the Shade. What if Niles is a plant? He certainly looks like a lot of those dark witches. Pale and malnourished. What are they feeding those guys anyway?"

"That's the dark magic taking its toll on their bodies," Hudson informed me. "I've dealt with dark witches and wizards before, they always look like that. It only gets worse with time. I'll keep an eye on Niles. I still keep an eye on Blake, even though I trust him now. What's your plan for the rest of the day?"

"I don't know," I said, drumming my hands on my thighs as I tried to remember whatever it was I did when I wasn't being hunted by dark wizards. "Go back to the bakery I guess, or something else?"

"How's the case going, the one with the murdered therapist? We could look into that together some more," he suggested.

"Hey, not a bad idea actually. I've not had a lot of chance to follow the case up. I'll call the station and see how they're getting on with things." I pulled out my phone and dialed the station. After a few rings Linda answered.

"Zora Wick, how do you do?! I've got a beauty for you. Seven down—"

"Linda, I said I'm not doing crossword puzzles anymore. Put Burt on the line," I said.

"Oh, come on, Wick! Not even for old time's sake?" Linda said in exasperation.

"Sorry Linda, dem's da rules now. Now put me through to Burt."

"Spoil sport," Linda muttered before transferring me over.

"Wick, that you?" Burt said and picked up the phone.

"Sure is. How's the case going? Made any progress yet?"

I heard Burt lean back in his chair and plonk his feet on the table. "Not so much. I'm still thinking the fiancé and this hobo were in on it together somehow, but I just can't piece it. The answer will come to me any day now. We didn't find anything at Howard's place, and the tracks didn't match his bike, but I'll figure it out."

I pulled the phone away from my ear for a moment and mouthed the words 'No progress' to Hudson. He just shook his head and smiled. "What about the tip the fiancé gave?" I asked.

"What tip would that be?" Burt said in confusion.

"The one about the childhood friend?" I recalled. "Glen something. Glen…" For the life of me I couldn't remember.

"Glen Atkins!" Burt said. "Gosh darn it I knew there was something I was meant to be doing! I have his name written on a post-it-note and stuck to my computer monitor. Couldn't remember who he was for the life of me!"

I let a moment of disbelief pass before proceeding. "After this case I think we all need to sit down at the station and talk about basic organization skills."

"You know what, Wick, I think that might just be a fine idea," he said earnestly. "I don't suppose you'd be interested in chasing up this Glen Atkins fellow for us, would you?"

"Why not?" I asked. "It's just a normal day in Compass Cove, and I'm acting normally, doing the things I'd normally do."

"…If you say so Wick. Get a pen and paper, I'll give you this fella's details. Or I could fax them over if it's easier?"

"Sure Burt, let me hop into my time machine, travel back into the eighties and receive your fax."

"Alright Captain Sassy, pen and paper it is. You ready?"

I opened up the notes app on my phone and put Burt on speaker. "I've inked my quill and unrolled my parchment. Where do I find this guy, Burt?"

* * *

"Who is this guy again?" Hudson asked as he drove us to the address.

"Glen Atkins. According to Helen's fiancé, Howard Price, he's been best friends with Helen since they were both kids and Howard says, and I quote, *He's always been kind of obsessed with her.*"

"That's why he's a suspect?" Hudson said, turning to look at me.

I shrugged. "Hey pal, I'm just going off what we have. Out of the two suspects so far, we haven't had any hot leads."

"Run it all by me," Hudson suggested. "I want to mull it over in my head. What are our clues?"

"A rare pollen was found at the scene. The killer fled on motorbike. They used a chisel as the murder weapon, and they left a threatening note with an error a few days before, spelling the word *cemetery* wrong."

"Okay, and the suspects?"

"Sure. The first guy is Oscar Mendel, 'The Carpet King'."

"Ah yes." Hudson smiled fondly. "The hot head who had his kids taken away, because of Helen's professional evaluation. He's got the motive... and the temper."

"He drives a car though, and there's no connection to the pollen, *or* the murder weapon."

"He did refuse to leave a handwriting sample though," Hudson pointed out. "Pretty suspicious if you ask me."

"Not really," I countered. "The guy was well within his rights to tell us to walk, plus you riled him up something fierce."

Hudson grinned back at me. "Yeah, I guess I did push him a little too far, huh? What was the fiancé like?"

"Considering he disappeared a day after the fact, he came out of that interview looking pretty clean. There's no connection to the murder weapon, and he passed the handwriting test. But he does drive a Vespa, and he does own a flower shop."

The brows on Hudson's head raised high. "Zora, come on! A flower shop? Strange pollen found at the scene? How is that guy not suspect number one? Especially after running."

"That's the thing, he didn't run. He left a message for Zayne at the station and told him where he was going, Zayne was just too lazy to check his messages."

"And then there's this third guy, the childhood friend that was possibly crushing on her," Hudson said.

And get this, Glen Atkins worked as a carpenter, Hudson and I were currently on our way to his workshop. "Possibly. All I know is that carpenters tend to have a lot of chisels…"

Hudson laughed to himself. "So let me get this straight. One suspect has an anger management problem and Helen essentially took his kids away. Strange pollen was found at the crime scene and her fiancé is a florist. And this stalker friend of hers is a carpenter and the murder weapon was a chisel?"

"That's about the long and short of it," I said. "What do you think?"

He let out a flustered sigh. "I have no idea. "I feel like it could be all of them… and none of them!"

I laughed. "Yeah. Well, let's see what Glen Atkins has to say," I said as we pulled into the lot connected to his workshop and store. Hudson parked up and we both headed into the shop, a small but bright room full of handmade furniture.

From the back of the building the smell of sawdust was strong in the air, and a table saw was buzzing away loudly. Hudson and I meandered through the shop to the register at the back and I rang a bell on the counter.

The sawing stopped and someone hollered through from the back. "Won't be a minute!" they shouted.

"Some of this stuff is really nice," Hudson said, turning around to admire a handmade baby crib on the ground next to us.

"Easy there sailor," I said, "We haven't even moved into together yet."

Hudson laughed and stood up, blushing slightly as he looked at me. "That's not what I was getting at."

"Why, what's wrong with my womb? Are you saying I'd be a bad mother?!" I said, feigning manic upset.

He was having none of it, Hudson came forward with a smile on his face and put his arm around me. "Not at all. You'd make a brilliant mother. Our fourteen kids will be beautiful."

Laughing, I pushed him off me and twirled out of his grasp. "Fourteen? It's not a clown car, Hudson, relax!"

He held his hands up in jest and winked. "I'm just proving that I can outmatch you in the crazy department, if not equal you at the least."

He definitely had me going for a moment.

"How can I help you folks?" a man said as he came out of the back. Turning around I saw a portly man with dark circles under his eyes.

"Glen Atkins?" Hudson asked, taking point.

"That's me, and this is my shop. How may I help you?"

"I'm Hudson Beck, and this is Zora Wick. We're investigators working with the police on the Helen Bowen murder case. We were hoping we might have a few minutes of your time and ask you some questions."

Glen Atkins went white as a sheet but nodded very slowly. "Of course," he stammered. "What did you want to know?" he asked, gently putting down a hammer on the counter. Both Hudson and I eyed it carefully.

"Anything you might be able to tell us about Helen Bowen," I said. "From our understanding you were good friends. Is there a chance she might have confided something with you? Maybe mentioned that she was afraid of someone hurting her?"

Glen thought about it before shaking his head. "No, not really. To be honest with you Helen and I were a lot closer when we were younger. We've sorted of drifted apart over the years. Real life sort of comes along and gets in the way. You know what I mean?"

"All too well," Hudson said. "Did you know Helen's fiancé well?"

"Howard?" Maybe I was imagining it, but it looked like Glen bristled slightly. "Yeah, I met him a few times. He seemed like a nice enough guy. Helen was head over heels for him, so… I was happy she'd found someone."

"We heard that they argued about money, did you ever hear anything like that?" I asked.

"No, to be honest whenever I met Howard it was usually at a get together, and Howard and Helen were always in good spirits. They were the perfect couple, everyone loved them." Although Glen said the words with good intention there was an edge to his voice that made me wonder if Glen was jealous of what Howard and Helen had.

A SCONE TO PICK

"Forgive me if this question is out of sorts," Hudson said, "but did you two have a history together? You ever date?"

Glen laughed nervously and scratched his face. "No, unless we're including the five minutes we were married during recess that one time." He looked at me and I smiled back, remembering the silly games I used to play in elementary school.

"How would you describe your relationship? Just friends? Or did you want it to be something more."

A deflated sigh came from the large man. "It's no secret that I had a huge crush on Helen, I always did. But I never had the nerves to do anything about it, and to be honest I knew that she didn't feel the same away about me. She was always dropped enough hints, saying that she loved me like a brother and all that."

"Some guys might get angry about that kind of rejection," Hudson suggested.

Glen shrugged it off. "I don't think I've ever been angry about it. I've known Helen a long time, I let her go a long time ago, but I still loved her spirit. The fact that someone would just go and take her from us like that…" For a moment Glen looked off into the distance, and I was almost sure I saw his bottom lip wobble. "I'm sorry, I just hope that you catch whoever did it."

"We hope so too," I said with a genial smile. "Glen, if you don't mind, we'd like to run a few things by you, just cross-examination questions to rule you out as a suspect."

Glen did a doubletake and looked at me. "I'm a suspect?" he said, looking genuinely surprised.

"It's merely routine procedure," Hudson advised. "We both know you didn't do it, but we have to rule everyone out." In reality there was still every chance Glen might have been the one responsible, but Hudson and I were jostling him around a little psychologically, testing him to see how he reacted.

"Of course," Glen sputtered. "Well, what did you need to know?"

"Where were you on the night of Helen's death?" Hudson pressed.

"I was here, working in the shop until late. I had a commission that I had to get finished. A chest of drawers for one of my clients."

177

"Can anyone verify that?"

"Sure, I got two workers up there," he said, pointing to cameras mounted from the ceiling. "There's one in the workshop too."

"We'd love to have a look, if that's not too much trouble," Hudson asked.

Glen brought a laptop through from the back and sure enough the surveillance footage stored on there showed him working in the shop the night that Helen died. It was easy to fake the timestamps on these kinds of things of course, but it was a big plus for his alibi.

"There's also a gas station across the road, one of its lot cameras catches my store. I know because someone dinged my truck last year and the gas station camera helped me catch the sucker."

Hudson and I gave each other a look, one that basically said, *okay, so the surveillance footage can be verified by someone else.* Glen could easily manipulate his own tapes, but the gas station across the road? Unlikely.

"I drive a truck myself," Hudson said. "Bike too. You a piston head?"

"Sorry, not really," Glen said with an amiable smile. "To me a truck is just a way of getting where I want to be. You wouldn't catch me dead on a bike, those things scare the heck out of me."

That ruled the bike out then. I had to try and find a connection to the other clues, if there was one. "Helen's fiancé was a florist, right?" I said to Glen.

"Uh, I think so…" he said. "Does that have something to do with the case?"

I faked a clumsy laugh. "Actually, I'm thinking out loud. Thought I might swing by the shop and see what his stock is like. Have you been?"

Glen shook his head. "No, I've got pretty severe allergies. I try and stay inside most of the summer. A florist is the last place I want to be."

"Say," Hudson said, swiftly moving to our next clue. "Do you mind if we had a look at your workshop?"

"Sure thing," Glen said, gesturing for us to step around the counter and into the back. The workshop was about the same size as the shop

A SCONE TO PICK

in the front, but filled with countertops, machines of all kinds, scrap pieces of wood and half-built pieces of furniture.

Hudson wandered one way around the workshop, while I walked the other. "Are you looking for anything in particular?" Glen asked. I glanced back to see that he was still waiting by the door.

As it happened Hudson and I both came across the thing we were looking for at the same time, stopping in front of a wall were tools of all shapes and sizes, hanging from hooks.

Hudson let out a low whistle. "Nice chisel collection you've got here. Full set," he turned and gave me a knowing glance. No missing murder weapon belonged here.

"Yup, a good carpenter always takes pride in keeping stock of his workshop," Glen said, sounding more and more confused with each of our seemingly abstract questions. I gave Hudson a nod to indicate I was satisfied with our findings, or lack thereof, and we walked back over to Glen. On the way I pulled the case file out of my bag and opened it to find the photo of the murder weapon.

"Do you have any chisels like this in your workshop?" I asked.

Glen squinted at the picture for a moment and then pulled his head back. "That's not a chisel," he said.

Hudson and I both looked at the photo. "I beg your pardon? What is it then?"

"I don't know," Glen said and shrugged. "But it's sure as heck isn't no chisel. It doesn't look sharp enough, and the handle to blade ratio is all wrong. I've seen a lot of tools over the years working in my shop, but never anything like that."

Huh. So, our murder weapon *wasn't* a chisel.

"Is there anything else I can help with?" Glen asked. "I really have to get back to work."

"Before we go, I'd like to trouble you for a quick handwriting sample, but then we're out of your hair."

Glen was happy enough to give the handwriting sample, and sure enough the spelling of cemetery was correct. He wasn't the person behind the threatening note. Hudson and I said our goodbyes, made our way back to the car and pulled away.

"Well," Hudson said, his hands turning over the wheel. "It seems like he has feelings for Helen, but his alibi is tight enough. People kill out of love all the time but is Glen Atkins our man? I'm not so sure."

"No, me neither. And we've been looking at our murder weapon wrong this whole time. If it's not a chisel than what is it?" A few silent seconds passed before I tried to shake the question out of my head.

"Any chance this is one of your eureka moments where you crack the whole case?" Hudson asked.

"Take me out for lunch first. Maybe the eureka moment will come after that."

Hudson laughed. "So that's how it is, huh? I guess I'll take the bait."

Now I just had to solve a puzzling question: when is a chisel not a chisel?

CHAPTER 22

It seemed the investigation had hit a wall, and with no other current leads to follow, I headed back to the police station and let Burt know how things were going down so far. Hudson and I kissed goodbye as he went back to work as well. After chatting with Burt, I stopped by the cells to talk with Saxophone Joe. On my way there I heard saxophone music echoing through the hallways.

"They let you have that thing in here?" I asked Joe with bemusement as I stopped in front of his cell. Joe carefully set his saxophone in its case and came over to greet me.

"As it happens the Sheriff is a sax fan. Can't say I'm too happy about being behind these bars, but I'm happy to have my axe with me, that's for sure. How are you doing, Miss Wick?"

I sighed slightly. "To be honest Joe I'm not great. I should have gotten you out of here by now, but I've been so caught up with other business in my life. Things are hectic at the moment, and I'm sorry. I am going to get you out though; I promise you that."

Joe smiled sadly. "I know you are Miss Wick, though I admit I'm starting to get a little worried. Sheriff Burt says they're going to be officially filing charges at the end of this week. I know I didn't do this, but the second I'm up there in front of a room full of white people... let's be honest, my chances are shot to heck."

"You don't have to worry about that, because it's not going to happen, I promise. I'm working this, Joe. I've already interviewed three different suspects, and I'll go over the evidence all over again, even if I have to stay up the rest of the week!"

Joe laughed. "I admire the determination, but I wouldn't skip on the sleep. My friend Cotton Corn Bob did that, and he went crazy, stripped naked and ran into traffic."

I stared at Joe for a moment as I processed that story. "M'kay then, I'll be sure to keep up with the forty winks. Is there anything I can get you in the meantime? Anything to make you more comfortable?"

"No ma'am," he said with a polite shake of the head. "I've got my axe, that's everything I need. Good luck, Miss Wick, I know you'll figure it out."

I left Joe and made my way back to the apartment, where I found a large oiled-up musclebound Latino man splayed across the couch, watching Spanish TV Novellas. I reacted by screaming, dropping my things on the floor and pulling out a wand, ready to attack.

"Who are you and what are you doing in my house?!" I screamed.

The shiny-skinned Latino man looked over at me and smiled confidently. "Hello darling," he said in a thick accent. "How was your day?"

"Get out of my house! Now!" I shrieked.

A confused look crossed the oiled-up man's face and he looked down at himself. An expression of understanding came over him. "Ah, my mistake," he said. Suddenly shimmering sparks of lights passed over his body, transforming him into the more familiar figure of my mother. "Sorry darling, I forgot I was dressed up as Fernando."

I narrowed my eyes at her. "Who now?"

"I was in disguise. I am hiding out until the Sisters of the Shade are dealt with. Fernando is one of my covers. It's a type of magic called skin shifting—quite difficult, but I'm sure I could teach it to you."

"But you're in my apartment. Why do you need a disguise?"

Mom pointed lazily at the large glass windows at the end of the apartment. "Your father has spies everywhere darling. They could peep through windows. It's not worth the risk." With that she snapped her fingers and another shower of sparks passed over her, transforming her into an elderly looking woman in a teal shell suit.

"So, you're like, seriously good at magic then?" I asked her, walking across the room to sit down beside her.

"Where do you think you get it from, honey? I always knew my daughters would be fantastic witches."

"I'm not that good, I still have a lot to learn," I pointed out.

"The important thing is to remember your raw talent," Mom said. "You're barely into your education Zora, and you're already running circles around witches with a lot more experience."

"Is it a genetic thing?" I asked. "You're prismatic. Is that why I ended up being prismatic too?"

"To be honest that surprised even me. There are other prismatic witches out there, but none of them have given birth to daughters with the same type of power. We may be the first, and it might have something to do with your father's natural abilities too."

I shuddered for a moment, wondering what else I might have inherited from the man. My memory flashed back to my last magic lesson with Amos, and his warnings of not falling into the path of dark magic temptation.

Mom seemed to notice my concern. "What is it? Your face looks all sad and forlorn."

"I'm just thinking about something my magic teacher told me. Do you think I have the ability to turn bad, like dad did?"

She raised a brow. "Is that what your teacher told you? That you're going to turn bad?"

"No, he just warned me about it. I guess it's been playing on my mind, especially so since I found out who my real father is."

"Your father was a good man when we were together," she reminded me. "He only turned bad when he was corrupted by the dark amulet, the same one that holds him prisoner to this day. It is a dangerous artefact full of dark and powerful demon magic, one that even the purest of minds would find hard to resist."

"You resisted it though," I pointed out. "You were in close proximity to it twice, and you only thought of destroying it, not taking it for yourself."

"I suppose you're right. Though I imagine if I'd found it first and I was by myself, it might me hunting you down now, and your father helping you out. Who can say?" she said with a shrug.

"I think you're being humble," I said, taking my ringing phone out of my bag.

Mom faked a look of disgust. "Am I? Oh goodness. Don't tell anyone. You'll ruin my reputation."

I laughed and stood up to take the call, it was from my cousin Sabrina.

"Hey, what's up?" I asked.

"Could I like, get your help with something?" she asked, faint struggling sounds happening in the background.

"Uh, sure. Is everything okay?"

"Yeah. I've got this irritating magical artifact and it's malfunctioning all over the place. I think I need to hit it with a serious bit of magic, and you're just about the strongest witch in town. Can you give me a hand?"

"I'll be right there," I said with a sigh. "I'm going to need cake afterwards though."

"Way ahead of ya, I've already got one sorted!"

***

I GATHERED up my things and ran over to Sabrina's shop to see what all the fuss was about. I was about halfway there in my van when I realized that someone was following me—or at least appeared to be.

To test out the theory I looped around the block and sure enough the car followed. It was an ugly little brown thing that looked like it was close to falling apart. As I reached Sabrina's shop and pulled into a spot the brown car did too. I hopped out of the van and secretly got my wand ready in case this had something to do with the Sisters of the Shade.

Upon closing the door and seeing the driver of the brown car I put away my wand and any notion of getting into a magical battle in broad daylight. The man driving the car was Kenny King, the slimeball public defender that I'd bumped into several times. The last time we'd met he was taking photos of Hudson and me on the night of Helen's murder.

I recalled Niles mentioning that Kenny had been following me. I was about to find out why. Without hesitating I marched over to Kenny's ugly brown car and threw open the driver door. He was hiding behind a newspaper but shrieked as I snatched it away.

"Hey, what's the big idea?!" he said in his thick jersey accent.

"Why are you following me?" I growled.

"I don't know what you're talking about, it's a small-town Miss Wax! People bump into one another all the time. You can't prove anything!" Kenny laughed nervously as an old man passed us by and sped up.

"It's Miss *Wick*, you imbecile! You know I'm pretty cozy with the local police, right? It wouldn't take much to get a restraining order put out against you. Maybe I could even get them to throw you in a cell for the night for stalking me—that counts as harassment you know? Wouldn't look good for a public defender to have that on his record."

"Hey, easy now, easy now! That's my livelihood you're talking about there!" Kenny said, getting out of the car with his hands held up. He was a bundle of frantic energy, his small black eyes constantly darting about all over the place. If Kenny hadn't gone into law, I could quite easily imagine him selling lemons on a dealership forecourt or ripping old people off with overpriced repair quotes.

I guess you could say the guy just had a real slimeball vibe.

"Start talking then, I said through my teeth. It was then that I noticed a camera on his passenger seat. "You're taking photos of me? Why?!"

"I'm trying to get clients. I've been hoping I can represent the people you've been meeting with on this case, but none of them want to bite!" he explained.

"So, you're following me so that you can find clients who might need legal representation?" I clarified.

"Exactly! I don't know if you noticed lady, but you're constantly in the thick of things, and old Kenny's black book is pretty empty these days. You rustle up a suspect, I sweep in after and see if they need a lawyer. The carpet guy, the florist, the carpenter. Kenny went to see them all, but no one is playing ball!"

"So, you're not chasing ambulances, you're chasing an independent investigator. I don't know if that's genius or an entirely new low," I surmised. God, I hated this guy.

Kenny gave another one of his weaselly grins and laughed. "Hey, I told you it wasn't insidious! Kenny's not a peeping tom!"

"What's with the camera then?" I asked. "You don't need that to harass suspects."

"Nope, but I can sell their pictures to the paper. My sister pays me a good fee and every story needs a face to it."

"There's always an angle with you, isn't there?"

"Hey, I've got seven kids to feed, you gotta put food on the table."

"You have seven kids?" I asked, mostly surprised this man had tricked a woman into sleeping with him once, let alone seven times.

"Don't act so surprised, they're my moon and stars, take a look!" Kenny pulled out his wallet and a stream of photos concertinaed out. I leaned in to get a closer look and pulled my head back.

"These are all photos of cats," I said flatly.

"To *you* it might just be a cat," he said with a note of offense, quickly folding up the photos and putting his wallet back in his pocket. "Now seeing as we're friends can I get a quote for the paper?"

"Why on earth would I do that? And we're not friends."

"Let's make a deal. You give me a quote and I'll stop following you. Scout's honor!"

"No way you were a scout," I said, folding my arms.

"Nah, they kicked me out for stealing the scout master's wallet, but in my defense he had it coming."

"Here's a deal. Give me all the photographs you've taken so far and leave me alone, then I'll give you a quote," I bargained.

"Hey, a deal's a deal, not the negatives though. This story might go big, and I need to have copies ready in case this thing goes national." Kenny leaned into his car and pulled an envelope out of the glove compartment.

"Yeah, I'm sure this small-town murder is going to hit the mainstream news any moment now," I said sarcastically. Kenny put the thick envelope of photographs into my hands, and I put it in my bag. "Okay," I said, brushing my fringe out of my face. "What quote do you want?"

"Why do you think Saxophone Joe killed Helen Bowen, and how long is he going away for?" Kenny asked, thrusting a voice recorder into my face.

I peeled back and pushed the recorder away. "If that's your attempt at a gotcha question it's bad," I said. "And Saxophone Joe is innocent. He's not going anywhere. Mark my words, end of quote." With that I turned and walked back in the direction of Sabrina's shop. "And remember to leave me alone!" I shouted back to him. "I don't want to see you again!"

"You don't need to worry about that!" Kenny said assuredly. "You won't!"

Somehow, I wasn't so sure. Kenny King was like the terminator of sleazeball lawyers.

I could run that guy over with a sixteen-wheel truck only for him to get back up again. If a nuclear bomb ever dropped on this town the only thing left would be cockroaches and Kenny King, and once the cockroaches realized who they were stuck with they'd get the heck out of town too.

As I headed for the front door of Sabrina's shop my phone started ringing again. Yeesh, what now?

"Zora? It's Tamara, Tamara Banana? The town CSI."

"Yes, believe it or not I don't know any other people called Tamara Banana. What's up?"

"I'm calling back because I got those pollen samples returned from Virginia. Get this, I know where the pollen is from!"

CHAPTER 23

"Guatemala?" I repeated. "Are you sure?"

"Positive. It's the *Orquidea Roraima*, otherwise known as the White Handed Flower. It's rare, like super rare, and it can only be found there," Tamara explained.

"So, I should check Howard's shop and see if they stock that flower..." I said, thinking out loud.

"No need," Tamara replied. "The *Orquidea Roraima* has very specific growth needs. It requires narrow temperature and humidity windows and the weather here would not cut it. Any florist wanting to make a profit wouldn't bother importing a flower like that."

"Huh, well, I'll call to double check, but I guess that only leaves me with more questions. It means our killer went to Guatemala recently?"

"That's right. Apparently, the pollen is quite unique, microscopic and very difficult to get off the skin. It can take weeks to completely remove trace of it from the body."

"Alright Tamara, thanks for the heads up. It's appreciated. Message me the name of that flower and I'll double check with Howard's shop."

"Will do!"

I made my way inside Sabrina's shop and heard her shouting from upstairs. "Up here! Quickly!" she said. Worrying that she might be in trouble, I ran up the stairs and stopped at the top to find Sabrina on the floor, bound from head to toe in black cord.

"What happened here?" I asked slowly.

"Stupid magic rope!" she snapped, shuffling around on the floor. "It's supposed to be half-sentient and follow instructions, but when I was putting it on the shelves this one sprang open and started wrapping itself around me!"

"You really need to stop buying these malfunctioning items," I said. Sabrina's shop operated on a rather... unique business model. She bought faulty stock from businesses that enchanted magical items. Sometimes the enchantment process didn't always go to plan and resulted in objects that produced strange and sometimes unknown effects. Sabrina bought those duds and sold them here in her shop.

"Yeah, you might be onto something there. Can you just get this thing off me? Blast it with a bit of force magic, and then we can try and rassle it back into the box."

Getting the rope off Sabrina was easy enough, one swipe of my wand and it came undone instantly. The hard part was catching the rope and getting it back in its box. What followed was a fifteen-minute slapstick chase across Sabrina's shop, finally ending when we managed to trap the elusive magic rope in an old hat box.

After catching my breath and promising Sabrina that I would never help her again, we both went into her apartment at the back of the shop and had some cake and tea. "How are things anyway," she asked. "You know, what with all the *stuff* happening recently."

"You mean my mom coming back and learning all the sordid secrets about my past? And that my real dad is coming to kill me?" I shoved a slice of cake into my mouth and chewed.

"Yeah... that stuff."

I shrugged. "I'm taking each day as it comes. How about you?"

"I suppose I'm ready to fight if I have to. Zelda was saying that you mentioned something about traitors?"

I nodded and swallowed the cake before attempting to speak. "Yeah, according to that Chang guy, there are three of them." Sabrina said nothing, but she brushed one hand up and down her arm and stared at the coffee table. "What's wrong?" I asked her. "I get the feeling you're not telling me something."

"It's nothing, well—" Sabrina smoothed her fingers over her brows and looked at me. "It's that Niles guy, you know, the one that Celeste has been dating?"

"Like, multiple dates?" I asked. "They've been out more than once?"

"Yeah, didn't she tell you? They're like, all over each other. It's crazy how fast things are moving. She told me she thinks he might be the one," she said, a note of concern on her face.

"And what do you think?" I asked.

"I don't know. I'm not sure about the guy. I've only met him once or twice, and you have to admit, he's definitely weird."

"Hey, no need to play it soft with me. That guy is a weapons grade weirdo. I've been saying it from the beginning. He's hiding something." I picked up another slice of cake and sailed it towards my mouth.

"Exactly! That's how I feel. Like he's hiding something. And what's even weirder is Celeste. I don't know if you've noticed, but she's been acting weird ever since he came on the scene. I think he's draining her or something. She's like, tired all the time, and she doesn't look well." Sabrina held her cup in her hands, but she hadn't taken a drink since we'd started talking.

"He's using her?" I asked. "Like… draining her spirit or something? Is that a thing?"

Sabrina shrugged. "I don't know, but I think we need to confront him. All of us. If there's a traitor amongst us, my money is on Niles."

"We have to be careful though, what if we're wrong? Celeste really seems to like this guy, and she wouldn't be happy if we barged in and did something big and embarrassing," I said.

"If we're wrong then I'll take the heat," Sabrina said. "I'd rather risk Celeste being mad at me than getting hurt because of this creep. She asked me to meet them at the diner tomorrow for lunch. She wants me to get to know him better."

"Alright. Let's all talk to her tomorrow then?" I suggested. "I can let Zelda know too."

Sabrina nodded, she looked relieved, but still nervous about the whole thing. "What are you up to now? Want to help me in the shop?"

"If you don't mind, I might stay here and read over some of the case notes. I've also got some photographs to look through. I've really hit a dead end with it all. It feels a little aimless at the moment."

"Stay as long as you want, it'll be nice to have the company. Do you want another cup of tea?"

"Yeah, and maybe more cake while you're at it," I said, looking at the empty plate on the coffee table. Sabrina had already brought over a small chocolate cake, but the poor little thing didn't stand a chance against the two of us.

"I think you might be a mind reader. I'll be right back."

Sabrina returned with more cake and popped out again to see to some customers in the shop. I cleared the coffee table and laid out my notes from the case and the photographs acquired from Kenny.

There were about one hundred photographs in all, and most of them were junk. Half of them weren't even in focus, and the other half were obscured by part of his fingertip. "Learn to use a camera, Kenny, sheesh," I muttered to myself.

As I came to the end of the photographs, I found a crisp and clear image of the street outside Helen Bowen's office. Wayne and Zayne were keeping guard outside the front doors, so it had to be just after Helen had died. Underneath this there was one more image, taken from the inside of Kenny's car. It looked like he was parked up on a street several blocks away, and he'd taken a photo of a dirt bike speeding past. Its rider was a larger man wearing a helmet.

"Kenny King you slimeball… I could actually kiss you." Or not, that would be disgusting. I pulled out my phone and called Kenny, still having his number after he briefly represented me when falsely accused of murder.

"Kenny King, speaking! Attorney at Law, crime scene photographer, and Children's Bounce House hire!"

"You're hiring out Bounce Houses now?" I said, momentarily blindsided by his greeting. "You might be the weirdest person I've ever met."

"Miss Wax!" he said endearingly. "Or should I say, Miss… *Wick?*"

"You should, seeing as it's my actual name. I need to ask you a question about these photographs. The photograph at the bottom of the stack, you're sitting in your car, and you've taken a picture of a dirt bike speeding past. Why?"

"Ah, that was just after the murder news came through on my police scanner. I fired a picture off to start a new reel of film and then I drove on over!"

"But why the dirt bike?" I asked.

"I don't know," Kenny said. "It came screaming down the road and I pointed and clicked. To be honest I was just starting a new reel. I wasn't really taking a picture of anything in particular."

Poor old Kenny didn't even realize he'd captured a photograph of the murderer fleeing the scene. There was no face visible because of the helmet, but there *was* a partial plate. "Alright Kenny. Let it be known that you might have actually done something useful for once. Bye!"

"What? Miss Wax? What did I do?!" he asked, but I hung up before I heard anymore.

Straightaway I called the police station, Linda answering after a few rings. "Can't you even help me with one little crossword clue?" she said desperately.

"Tell you what, do something for me and I'll be back on crossword assistance. It's to do with the Helen Bowen case. I've got a picture here showing a partial plate on the murderer's getaway vehicle. Can you run it for me?"

"I can, it might take a while with a partial plate though. What have you got?"

"The last three digits. They're 0GX."

"Alrighty, leave it with me, Wick. I'll call back when I find something."

I put my phone down beside me and turned my attention back to the photographs and files sprawled across Sabrina's coffee table. The final puzzle piece was in here somewhere, I just knew it. But where?

After half an hour of searching over notes I found myself slumped on the sofa, staring at the photograph of the murder weapon. The chisel that wasn't a chisel. Sabrina came through the door that led to her shop and sighed.

"Boy, talk about a nightmare customer. I've just been walking that woman around my shop for an hour and had to answer like a million questions." Sabrina went over to the kitchen and turned the kettle on.

"Did she buy anything?" I asked.

"Oh yeah, she spent a *chunk*, but I really had to work for it, you know? I prefer those easy sales. Want a cup of tea?"

"Go on then," I sighed, angling the photograph slightly, as if viewing it slightly askew might clear up some answers.

"What have you got there? Sabrina asked.

"This is the elusive murder weapon in the case. We thought it was a chisel, but apparently that's not the case."

Sabrina walked over to inspect the photograph. "Nah, that's not a chisel. Looks like someone has been putting down carpet though."

I put the picture down very slowly and turned around to look at Sabrina. "What did you just say?"

"Carpet. That's a tool for tucking in carpet between the floor and wall. I did my own carpet fitting because those cowboys cost and arm and a leg."

I stood up very quickly as the last puzzle piece fell into place. "Sabrina, you beauty! You just blew this whole thing wide open!"

"I did?" she asked, looking very puzzled as I gathered up my things and ran for the door.

There was only one last thing to do: apprehend the murderer.

* * *

"You sure you're right about this?" Sheriff Burt asked me as he climbed out of his cruiser. I'd already been in the lot for five minutes, waiting for backup.

"Positive. Are Wayne and Zayne in position?"

Burt nodded. "They are. You're sure this guy will run?"

"They always do," I said. "Come on, let's go inside."

Burt and I headed inside, and we saw our man pretty much straightaway. He was with a customer, flicking through a dense book of carpet samples.

"Oscar Mendel!" I announced. He turned and looked in our direction. "You are under arrest for the murder of Helen Bowen. Anything you say and—"

Quick as a flash Oscar Mendel hurled the heavy book of carpet samples in our direction and started sprinting towards the back of the store. Burt and I looked at one another with a knowing smile and followed at a leisurely pace. Mendel burst through a set of fire doors that led out of the back of the building and ran straight into Wayne and Zayne, who were actually in the right place for once, doing their job.

Despite their poor organizational skills, Burt's sons were both large guys, and had no problem pinning down Oscar Mendel and cuffing him. Mendel tried to fight, of course he did, but before long he knew the jig was up. He stopped struggling with a defeated sigh and stared daggers at me.

"I'm innocent. You can't prove anything!" he spat.

"Yeah, innocent people don't tend to do much running," I pointed out. "And the evidence is overwhelmingly stacked against you. The murder weapon wasn't a chisel at all, it was a carpet tucker, and I have a funny feeling I know where you found one of those."

"That could have been anyone's!" he said. "It's nothing! It'll never hold up!"

"Maybe not on its own, but there's also the strange pollen we found at the scene, which can only be traced back to a rare flower in Guatemala, which just happens to be the location of the fishing trip you recently took with your brother."

Wayne and Zayne lifted Oscar to his feet and started walking him back in the direction of the cruiser. Mendel just laughed. "Do you know who I am? You're going to need more than that! I'm the Carpet King! Everyone loves me around here! I'm innocent, innocent!"

"I'm sure you are," I said sarcastically. "You'll need to explain why someone snapped a picture of you speeding away from the scene on a dirt bike though. I recall you mentioning briefly that you used to ride. And of course, the last piece of evidence is the threatening note you left anonymously on Helen's car a few days before you murdered her. You refused to give a handwriting sample, and we both know why."

It was at that point, halfway to the cruiser, that Mendel's anger finally exploded. He turned and screamed at me until he was red in the face. "She took my kids away! What did she think would happen! It all came down to her opinion, and she made me out to be some sort of hot-headed lunatic, one that scares his wife and kids! Yeah, I killed that cretin, and I'd kill her again in a heartbeat! And once I get out of prison, I'm going to kill you too!"

An awkward silence passed between us all momentarily and Oscar Mendel paused, realizing that his anger had gotten the best of him once again. Burt just chuckled to himself and shook his head.

"Alright boys, get this one down to the station and lock him up. This case is closed."

I watched as Wayne and Zayne put Oscar into the back of cruiser but stopped them before they shut the door. "Wait! One last thing! Why did you frame Saxophone Joe?"

Oscar looked at me and shrugged. "The bum in the park? I don't know. I drove past there on my way home, and I planted the pendant on him. It was nothing personal, I just needed someone else to take the fall."

I shook my head and closed the door to the cruiser, signaling to Wayne and Zayne that they could leave.

"Well Wick, you did it again," Burt said. "We'll have your friend freed immediately, though I must confess I'm going to miss that sweet saxophone music floating through the police station." Burt gave me an affectionate pat on the back and then walked back over to his cruiser. "Another successful case for Bread Herring Inc!" he shouted.

"That's not the name of my investigation business!" I shouted back. Though to be honest I hadn't come up with anything better myself.

It was time to go home, put my feet up and finally relax.

Another case closed.

CHAPTER 24

Three weeks had passed since closing the Helen Bowen case. During that time things in Compass Cove had returned to normal, or as normal as things could be in town. Blake still wasn't back from the woods, Hudson was staying over more regularly, and mom was still hiding out in my apartment, staying out of sight until the Sisters of the Shade made their next move.

There hadn't been any sign of the dark witches or my father in town, and I was still going through the motions of normal daily life, pretending that I wasn't ready to fight back at any moment in case of attack.

In fact, it was startingly easy to forget about the dark witches with every new day. Maybe my crazy father had a change of mind and turned his minions around, or maybe he was just waiting for that perfect opportunity.

For the most part I was working at the bakery and helping around town every now and then when people needed the assistance of a prismatic witch. My abilities were beginning to grow steadily, and my lessons with Amos were even gaining momentum too. He'd even started mentioning booking magical exams for the end of the year, which would mean I had the equivalent of a high school magical education—if I passed. That was a while away though, and right now I was happy growing the bakery and spending time with my friends and family.

It was a hot sunny day when Celeste reached out for my assistance in finding a rare type of mushroom in the forest bordering Compass Cove. The spot was apparently an hour's hike from the nearest parking lot, and apparently the mushrooms would be easier to find with my magical assistance.

"Just to be clear…" I panted as we hiked up a steep forest trail. "These magic mushrooms aren't *those* types of magic mushrooms, right?"

Celeste laughed. "No, they're actually magic. They're Wandilows. You grind them up and they make brilliant fertilizer for other magical herbs. I'm running really low," she said in a sort of monotone manner.

I cast a concerned look over at Celeste, who definitely hadn't seemed herself lately. She was pale, looked like she had lost weight, and not as upbeat as she normally was. We'd never got to confront Niles either because he'd fallen off the radar, rather mysteriously.

"How are things with you and Niles?" I asked, trying to open up a conservation I knew she might find exciting.

"I think they've come to an end…" she said despondently. "I haven't seen him for like a week now, and he doesn't even respond to my messages."

I knew that guy was a scumbag. "There are other fish in the sea," I said, trying to cheer her up. "You'll find someone."

"Yeah," she said, and then we fell back into silence again.

Not long after that we reached the top of the trail and Celeste led us off the path. "They grow just around here somewhere. Follow me."

"Man, we must nearly be at the town boundaries we've walked so far!" I joked.

Celeste didn't laugh or say anything in return, she just kept walking ahead a few paces. It was then that I noticed a very faint wall of gold light about fifteen feet ahead of us, running through the woods.

We *were* at the magical boundary.

"Wait a second..." I said, backing up as I saw another figure waiting for us in the woods. Celeste stopped in her tracks as she saw him too. Niles walked out of the shadows with his hands in his pockets. He didn't say anything at first.

"You?!" I said. Then I looked at Celeste, and the pieces started to click together in my head. "Celeste, did he make you bring me here?"

Celeste turned in my direction, but her eyes looked different now —all black, with no hint of white. "No," she said, her voice sounding choral. "The master did." Celeste pulled out her wand and pointed it at the boundary.

"No!" Niles shouted, and he launched across the clearing and tackled Celeste, but he wasn't fast enough. They both hit the ground, and something shot out of Celeste's wand, shattering a section of the golden boundary. The light was still there, but large cracks ran across the surface now and flickered. Beyond the flickering sections I saw a small group of dark witches grinning maniacally, waiting to get in.

"Get off me! Get off me!" Celeste roared in a voice that sounded demonic. I could only watch in horror as Niles struggled against her, trying to pin her to the ground. I was so confused my feet were planted to the floor.

"Don't just stand there!" he snapped at me. "Bind her! We need to get it off her now!"

"Bind *her*?!" I said in amazement. "You're the one doing this to her!"

"I'm trying to save you both, you idiot! Now are you going to help or stand there all day?!" The next thing Celeste delivered a kick to Niles' abdomen and sent him flying across the clearing. Okay, something weird was definitely going on here. I pulled out my wand and blasted Celeste with binding magic.

"Release me! Release me!" she screeched, frantically rolling around on the floor as she tried to break the binds. Niles jumped back to his feet and sprinted over to her, bent over and ripped something from around her throat. As he did the demonic fervor that had come over Celeste stopped immediately. She closed her eyes and passed out.

"What is that thing?" I asked Niles, staring at the necklace in his hand. He was breathing heavily, holding the item tight.

"The Sisters of the Shade took control of Celeste somehow. She's been the one letting them into town. She was the traitor."

"What? Impossible!" I gasped. "Celeste would never—"

"It was the necklace, you moron," Niles snapped. "It was controlling her against her will." He dropped it to the ground and crushed it under foot.

It was then that the boundary shattered, the two of us looked up and saw five Sisters of the Shade, running towards us with their wands outstretched. Beams of deadly magic light started flying in all directions, Niles grabbed me and pulled me to cover behind the nearest tree.

"Cover me!" he shouted. "I'll get Celeste!"

With little other choice I ducked out from behind cover as Niles ran to get Celeste. He could move fast, just like Blake, and blurred across the forest floor like a blurred ribbon of color. In a few seconds he was back again, having put Celeste safely on the ground behind me.

"We have to get out of here!" he said. "There's too many of them!"

"No," I growled. "They're not coming into my town. We fight."

I ducked out again and sent a shower of sparks straight into the eyes of a witch running for us. She hit the ground and didn't get back up. Two more ran around to flank us. "Over there!" I said to Niles. He sprinted off in one direction while I focused on the other witch.

A bolt of hot red light blasted into the tree next to me and sent splinters of wood flying everywhere. In retaliation I threw another bolt back and hit the witch, but just before she went down another shot fired off and caught me in the hip, dropping me to the ground.

I tumbled down a small dirt hill, pine needles and dry leaves crunching underneath me until I stopped at the bottom. Looking down I saw no blood, but my hip throbbed with pain, as though someone had punched it hard.

It was only when I went to grab my wand that I realized I was in trouble. Both my hands were bound together and encased with some sort of strange black goop. I couldn't fight these witches without my hands.

I pushed myself up to my feet and looked up to see two of the dark witches standing in front of me. "Do you surrender willingly?" one of them asked me.

"What do you think?" I sassed back.

"Then we offer our condolences."

Both of the witches sent bolts of violent red magic in my direction. I went to deflect the magic but before I could someone jumped across my path and took the hits—it was Niles.

He hit the ground and went immediately still, and then it was just me and the witches.

"Chivalrous, but to what end?" the other witch said. "He's dead, and now—" She lifted her wand. "So are you!"

With no way of defending myself I closed my eyes and braced for the end. I heard their deadly magic bolts fire through the air and then I heard something else: a high-pitched voice screaming.

"Don't worry Tony, we've got you!"

As I opened my eyes I saw hundreds of little red imps everywhere, running through the forest in their designer Italian suits and swarming the dark witches.

"They're everywhere!" one of the witches screamed.

"Run!" screamed the other. "Run!"

I could only watch in amazement as the two remaining dark witches attempted to flee, only to be subdued moments later by the imps that had come running to my aid. With my attackers all neutralized I found myself staring with my mouth open.

"What's up, Tony? You look like you've seen a ghost!" one of the imps said to me. I don't know how I could differentiate, but I knew it was the staircase imp.

"What on earth are you guys doing here?" I said, still trying to wrap my head around the fact that I'd just been saved by imps.

"Don't sound so surprised, Tony. We told you we were forever in your debt. You're Zora Wick, the great witch who handed us the infinite tabletop! I know you think we're a bunch of crooks, but I told you we weren't such bad guys! Bada bing?" he said. "Restore that boundary boys and then we're out of here!"

And so, it ended just like that. Although the imps and I had initially been enemies, I wouldn't have been alive without them, and it turned out that Niles actually was a good guy after all. Celeste woke up not long after the fight was over, and she had no idea where she was. Niles didn't wake, but he was breathing—somehow, he'd survived two bolts of killing magic.

"Wait? I was the traitor?!" Celeste said, her eyes brimming with tears as I caught her up to speed.

"It wasn't you; it was the necklace you were wearing."

"But still, I could have killed you!" she bawled. "And Niles, Niles, why won't he wake up! I've ruined everything!"

I tried my best to console Celeste, but obviously she was shaken by the whole thing. I made several calls after the fight was over, the first one was to Hudson, and the second was to the MCI.

It wasn't long before backup arrived, after which the imps said their goodbyes. The dark witches were apprehended, and Hudson ran up to give me the biggest hug. He wasn't alone, there were other MAGE members with him. They put Niles onto a stretcher and carried him through a portal.

"Can Celeste go?" I asked Hudson. "They're kind of an item."

"She can, but we'll have to blank her mind on the way back."

"Will he live?" I asked him after the portal closed.

"It's difficult to say. It looks like he was wearing some sort of protection, but two killing bolts? I've never heard of someone surviving that before. Come on, let's get you home. You've faced enough for one day."

And with that we made the way home. I was bruised, I was battered, but I'd lived to see another day, and foiled another attack from the dark witches.

One traitor down.

Two to go.

THANKS FOR READING

Thanks for reading, I hope you enjoyed the book.

It would really help me out if you could leave an honest review with your thoughts and rating on Amazon.

Every bit of feedback helps!

ALSO BY MARA WEBB

~ Ongoing ~

Hallow Haven Witch Mysteries

An English Enchantment

Compass Cove Cozy Mysteries

~ Completed ~

Wicked Witches of Pendle Island

Wildes Witches Mysteries

Raven Bay Mysteries

Wicked Witches of Vanish Valley

MAILING LIST

Want to be notified when I release my latest book? Join my mailing list. It's for new releases only. No spam:

Click here to join!

I'll also send you a free 120,000 word book as a thank you for signing up.

marawebbauthor.com

amazon.com/-/e/B081X754NL
facebook.com/marawebbauthor
twitter.com/marawebbauthor
bookbub.com/authors/mara-webb

Printed in Great Britain
by Amazon